Margaret Tempest.

LITTLE GREY RABBIT'S
STORYBOOK

LITTLE GREY RABBIT'S STORYBOOK

by Alison Uttley

PICTURES BY
MARGARET TEMPEST

Collins St James's Place London

William Collins Sons & Co Ltd
London · Glasgow · Sydney · Auckland
Toronto · Johannesburg

First published in this edition 1977
Copyright reserved
ISBN 0 00194162 3

Made and Printed in Great Britain by
William Collins Sons & Co Ltd Glasgow

Contents

Little Grey Rabbit's Party

One evening Hare came racing down the lane and
through the wicket gate to the little house at the end of
the wood. He was quite out of breath as he dashed into
the kitchen, where Squirrel and little Grey Rabbit sat.

"I took a short cut across the lawn of the farmhouse,
just now," said he. "I was going to watch Hedgehog
milking, but I heard a strange noise." He paused, waiting for their questions.

"Oh? What was it?" asked Squirrel, looking up from
her knitting. She picked up the ball of wool and put it
on the table. "What was it, Hare?"

"It was a party!" said Hare. "I stood up on tiptoes by
the juniper-bush, you know," – Squirrel and little Grey
Rabbit nodded excitedly, – "and I looked through the
window. I saw lots of little boys and girls bobbing up and
down, like, like, er—er——"

7

"Like rabbits on a common?" asked little Grey Rabbit.

"Like squirrels up a tree?" asked Squirrel.

"Like hares on the mountains," said Hare, frowning.

"And they played games and sang. I watched them, but they couldn't see me."

"Are they there now?" interrupted Squirrel, throwing her knitting on the floor, and springing up.

"Yes. I hurried home to tell you both. I raced like the North wind."

Little Grey Rabbit sat very still, but her eyes opened wide as she heard Hare's tale.

"Let's go and watch them," cried Squirrel. "We've never seen a party."

They dragged on their wraps and mufflers, and got ready in less than a minute. Little Grey Rabbit put a fire-guard round the fire, Squirrel locked the door, and put the key under a stone in the garden. Hare jumped up and down crying, "Hurry up! Hurry up! You'll be too late. Come along, do, Slowcoaches!"

He raced along with great leaps down the garden path, and Squirrel ran after, and little Grey Rabbit went as fast as she could, but as her legs were much shorter than Hare's, and she had not the speed of Squirrel, who often took short cuts, she was nearly left behind.

Down the fields they ran, through the stiles, along the narrow lanes, and under the five-barred white gate, where the old mare stood waiting to enter the stable. They ran across the drive to the lawn, and stood under the juniper-bush, staring in the twilight at the darkened house.

"I can't see anything," murmured Grey Rabbit sadly.

"Nor I," muttered Squirrel, running up the bush and down again.

"They've shuttered the windows," cried Hare, disappointedly, and they all gazed unhappily at the barred shutters. Little sounds of merriment, squeals and cries of joy came from the hidden room, and Grey Rabbit gasped as she listened.

Hare walked slowly round the corner of the gable, and Squirrel and Grey Rabbit trailed after.

Then Hare gave a shrill cry. "Here's a little window they've forgotten," said he. "Come and look here!"

Hare stood on tiptoes, Squirrel climbed on a rose-bush, and little Grey Rabbit scrambled on top of a wheelbarrow. In the warm, bright room they could see little boys and girls in party frocks and Sunday suits, playing Blind Man's Buff, and Hunt the Thimble, and Musical Chairs. Somebody hid the thimble on the window ledge quite near the faces of the peering animals, and Grey Rabbit got so excited she nearly screamed when a little girl found it.

Then the children trooped to another room for tea, and the animals got only a glimpse of the gay table through the open door, when a hand appeared and closed the shutter. They were left out in the cold.

"What do you think of that?" asked Hare, turning a somersault. "I found it! It was my discovery!"

"It was very clever of you," said Squirrel, but little Grey Rabbit said nothing. She sat in the wheelbarrow staring at the blank window. She took little short breaths and her eyes shone.

"Why don't you speak, Grey Rabbit?" cried Hare impatiently, and Grey Rabbit leapt down and trotted silently by his side. "Didn't you like it? Wasn't it wonderful?"

"Yes," whispered Grey Rabbit. "I was thinking, and wondering, and wishing. That's all."

Hare dashed off in front, and reached home first, but as he had forgotten where Squirrel had put the key, he was cold and cross when the others arrived.

"Do let's have supper," said he. "That party has made me hungry." So little Grey Rabbit filled the bowls with bread and milk, and they all sat round the table.

"Couldn't we give a party?" asked Hare, sipping from his spoon.

"Why not?" said Squirrel, and they both turned to the Rabbit.

"That's just what I was thinking about," said she, "but I don't know much about such things. That is the first party I have ever seen."

"Does it say anything about parties in your riddle

book, Hare?" asked Squirrel.

Hare reached down his green riddle-book, but although there were a hundred riddles, there was nothing about parties.

"You had better ask Wise Owl," said Squirrel. "He knows everything."

Grey Rabbit went pale. She hadn't seen Wise Owl for so long she was sure he had forgotten her.

"I don't think I mind very much about a party," said she faintly.

"Oh, do! Do! Little Grey Rabbit! He won't hurt you; you're a favourite of his," they both cried. So the next day Grey Rabbit went off with a pot of crab-apple jelly in her basket.

She ran through the wood in the dusk, and arrived at Wise Owl's tree just as the moon appeared.

"Ho! Wise Owl," cried she, and she rang the little silver bell beside the neat small door.

Wise Owl put his head out and looked down at her with great round eyes.

"Who's there?" said he fiercely, and then when he recognised the small rabbit, he asked, more gently. "What do you want, Grey Rabbit? You know it isn't safe in this wood after twilight. What do you want?"

"If you please, Wise Owl," said Grey Rabbit politely, "we, that is, Squirrel, Hare and I, want to give a party, and we don't know how, and we thought you could tell us."

12

"It's a long time since I was at a party," said Wise Owl musingly. "I forget whether it was a Christmas party, a birthday party, a tea party, or a Conservative party. But have you brought your present?"

Little Grey Rabbit held up the pot of jelly, and Owl, with a "Humph!" of approval, ate it all up.

"Yes, not so bad," said he. "You must invite me to your party," and he went back into the tree. Little Grey Rabbit sat waiting and wondering if he had finished, when the door of the beech-tree opened, and Wise Owl tossed a little red book from his library. "How to give a party," it was called.

"Don't thank me," he grunted, "but remember to send an invitation." He rose noiselessly and flew across the wood to his hunting, and Grey Rabbit pattered off home, with the book safe against her beating heart, and her little feet hurrying past all the dark holes, gloomy trees, and whispering rustling sounds with which the wood was filled at dark.

The Hare and the Squirrel seized the book as soon as she arrived, and buried their noses in it.

"Turn the Trencher. Blind Man's Buff. Hunt the Thimble," they read. "Come and explain all this to us, Grey Rabbit. You are the scholar. The words are so long."

Little Grey Rabbit sat by the fire, warming her toes and reading the party book, and Squirrel and Hare sat on either side of her crying, "Oh!" and "Ah!" and

"That's a fine game!"

All that week the three studied the little book, and made their plans. There were Forfeits, and Invitations, and Thimbles, and R.S.V.P. and Iced Cake to remember. Hare's fur nearly turned white with the strain on his memory.

"What is R.S.V.P.?" he asked, although Grey Rabbit had told him already.

"Rat Shan't Visit Party," said Grey Rabbit. "It is to make our guests feel at home."

"What is forfeits?" asked Hare. "It is something you have to do to get back something," said Grey Rabbit confusedly.

"Like giving the jelly to Wise Owl for this book," explained Squirrel in a motherly way.

" 'Cry in one corner, sing in another, dance in another, and laugh in another,' " read Grey Rabbit, and Hare muttered the words in a rigmarole as he walked about the garden, and did his daily work.

"I'll take charge of 'Turn the Trencher,' " said Hare. "I know where there is a grand trencher. It's a silver crown that Mole showed me once. He'll lend it to me when he hears about the party."

"I'll take charge of 'Blind Man's Buff,' " said Squirrel, "because I can knot the handkerchief. Remember how I tied Rat's tail."

"R.S.V.P. Rat Shan't Visit Party," murmured Hare. Then he said more cheerfully, "You'd better do the

14

refreshments, Grey Rabbit, and then we shall be sure of something good to eat. You must write the invitations, too. I'll get a new quill pen from the goose."

"Could we play Hide the Knitting Needle?" asked Squirrel. "Or Hide the Mince-pies?" inquired Hare, excitedly jumping from his chair.

"The party game is 'Hide the Thimble,'" said Grey Rabbit, looking again at the little red book.

The preparations began. Little Grey Rabbit went shopping, and came back with caraway seeds and candied peel, beech-nut flour and cinnamon sticks. Squirrel looked in the little store-houses under the trees, and brought hoards of nuts, which she ground in a stone bowl. Hare galloped across the common and brought a basket of eggs from the speckledy hen. There was such a mixing and stirring and tasting and trying, as little Grey Rabbit made her cakes and pies and custards, and Hare and Squirrel dipped in their paws!

Every morning Hare learned his forfeits as though they were lessons. "'Cry in one corner, laugh in another, sing in another, and dance in another,'" he repeated. "Grey Rabbit, Grey Rabbit, there's a stool in that corner. No one can dance there," he cried, and then, "Grey Rabbit, Grey Rabbit, what can they sing?"

He ran over the hard wintry fields and knocked at Mole's back door, banging with his furry knuckles, and kicking with his toes.

Mole put out his head, stuck his little snout in the air,

16

and asked, "What is the matter, Hare? Have you lost somebody? Is your house a-fire?"

"No," answered Hare, "I want to borrow that big silver coin of yours."

"Certainly," replied the obliging Mole, and he trundled it to the door, and held it with one paw against the door-post. "What do you want it for, Hare?"

"It's a secret," hesitated Hare, "but I'll tell you. We are giving a party, and this is for 'Turn the Trencher'. You are coming, you know. There are forfeits, – 'Sing in one corner, sit down in another, stand up in another, and go to sleep in another.' No, that's wrong. Oh, I've quite forgotten. I must ask Grey Rabbit. 'Laugh in one corner——' "

"Stop a minute," cried Mole. "You make me breathless. Tell me slowly."

"No, it's a secret," said Hare. "Good-bye till Party Day."

Away he went, rolling the silver coin down the little hills, pushing it up the slopes, towards home. Mole returned to his cellars, shaking his head. "Scatter-brained! Feather-pated!" said he to himself. "What did he mean by forfeits?"

On the way back Hare ran into little Fuzzypeg, who was hurrying home from school.

"Are you bowling a hoop?" asked Fuzzypeg.

"No, this is for 'Turn the Trencher,'" explained Hare. "We're giving a party, and you are invited. But it's a secret. 'Laugh in one corner, walk in another, talk in another and——'" Hare put his paw over his mouth. "I must be mum."

"Oh," cried Fuzzypeg. "Tell me more."

"No it's a secret," whispered Hare, and he ran on, trundling the silver crown with a little stick he picked up. By the time he had reached home he had told his secret to so many that it was no longer a secret, and all over the fields and woods and lanes and hedgerows the news spread that Hare was going to have a party, and there would be forfeits for tea, and everyone had to cry, or laugh, or sit, or stand in a corner.

"But what are forfeits?" asked every little rabbit in every little burrow.

"What are forfeits?" asked the cows in the sheds, who had been included in the general invitation.

"What is forfeits?" asked Old Hedgehog.

"A kind of Indian corn," said the Hens. "A kind of fodder," said the Horses. "A kind of nut," said the red Squirrels.

Each day little Grey Rabbit baked and brewed, and went to the market for fresh stores. She bought muslin for jelly bags, and ribbons for Squirrel's dress, and a neck-tie for Hare.

Squirrel and Hare collected sticks to make a big fire, to cook all the dainties, and they blew with the brown blow-bellows, to send a great flame up the chimney.

Little Grey Rabbit took the new goose quill and wrote

the invitations on sparkling holly-leaves.

"Squirrel, Hare, and Grey Rabbit
invite you to their party.
Full Moon Night.
Bring Mugs. R.S.V.P."

She gave the bundle of letters to the Robin, and asked him to deliver them. "Take one to Moldy Warp, and three to the Hedgehog family, and one to Toad and one to Wise Owl, and several to the Brown Rabbits, and the Squirrels," said she.

"But I invited the Cows and Horses," said Hare, "and the Pigs and Geese and Hens."

Grey Rabbit gasped. "Oh, Hare! How could we get them in our little house? Duchess, the Mare, would trample everything! You must tell them it was a mistake."

"I'll make it all right, Grey Rabbit," said the Robin. "I'm used to explaining. Postmen are Jacks-of-all-trades."

He counted the shiny leaves into his bag, fastened the buckle, and flew off, visiting holes, corners, and tiny huts, and popping one letter into a cranny of the beech-tree for the Owl.

The day of the party came. Squirrel, Hare, and little Grey Rabbit rose whilst it was still dark, there was so much to do. Squirrel practised tying knots in the big silk handkerchief. Hare turned the silver trencher, and repeated under his breath, " 'Cry in one corner, laugh in another.' " Little Grey Rabbit ran backwards and forwards, decorating the room with branches of red-berried holly, and delicate white mistletoe.

Across the middle of the room was the tea-table, with three mugs, and space for a dozen more when the guests arrived. There were pink cakes, and white cakes, and sponge cakes, and mince-pies, and sandwiches of potted cob-nuts, and roasted chestnuts. In the middle was the party cake, a great round cake covered with icing, which Hare had brought from the top of the pond. In the centre of it were tiny snow figures of a rabbit, a hare and a squirrel. Hare paused in his trencher-turning to admire the group which he had made.

"Very artistical," said he. "Won't people stare!"

When the full moon peeped out from the trees, the three went upstairs to dress.

Hare put on his best red coat, Squirrel wore her yellow dress, and tied her ruddy tail with a blue bow. Little Grey Rabbit was draped in a pale scarf of finely made cobweb which Hare had found in a corner of a barn. On her feet she wore her silver-birch slippers, Toad's present of long ago. In her pocket was a tiny lace handkerchief, exquisite embroidery made by the frost and rain from a lime leaf.

She looked through the window at the golden ball of the moon, and she watched a company of wild young

21

rabbits, dragging home some leafy branches of holly for a bonfire. They went round the corner, shouting, "Hi! Hi! Hi!"

Then they crept up to a window and peeped in at the feast.

Grey Rabbit ran downstairs and gave them each a rosy crab-apple, and a hot mince-pie, stuffed with herbs, and they shuffled their feet, and thanked her with shrill little voices.

"Who's that?" cried Hare. "Have they come? I'm not ready."

When the rabbits had gone, Grey Rabbit took a last look round to see if all was ready. She filled some bristly beech-nut boxes with pink sugar for the youngest squirrels and put aside a basket of walnut-shells, crammed with honey, for the field-mice who hadn't been invited.

Suddenly she heard a soft shuffle and thump, and she saw Rat's hungry eyes peering in. Rat was quite thin, for he had had no luck in his burglaries since he broke into Grey Rabbit's house and Squirrel tied the knot in his tail.

"R.S.V.P.," whispered Grey Rabbit, but she slipped outside with a herb-pie, and left it on a stone. Rat sidled up, snatched it, and ran off.

"Who's that?" cried Hare again, as he heard the thump! thump! of Rat's tail on the path.

Next came old Hedgehog, carrying a can of milk.

"I've come right early," said he. "I hope you'll excuse my smock, but I knew you wanted milk for the party, and I came straight from the cows. The Missis and Fuzzypeg are coming soon, but they are titivating themselves."

Little Grey Rabbit welcomed him in. He hung his yoke on a nail by the door, and sat down with his hands on his knees.

"My! You've made it champion!" he exclaimed, looking round.

There was a knock at the door, and Mrs Hedgehog and Fuzzypeg hurried in. Mrs Hedgehog wore her best silk dress, and Fuzzypeg had on new shoes that squeaked.

Mole, in black velvet, followed. He brought a box of blue beads for Grey Rabbit. "Dug 'em up, part of a treasure trove," said he, "and washed 'em in the brook, and threaded 'em on a hair from Duchess's tail."

Grey Rabbit thanked him, and held their coldness to her cheek. Then came the party of Brown Rabbits, and the family of Squirrels, all in a crowd, for they had travelled in company. Water Rat followed, slim and handsome in his starched frills. Toad sent a note declining the invitation, for it was too far from his home, and he was very sleepy.

"I'm sleepy, too," said the Hedgehog, "but I just rub my eyes and keep on going-on-doing."

"But where's Wise Owl?" asked Hare.

"Owl? Is he coming?" Everyone looked nervous, and

the youngest rabbit started for the door.

Little Grey Rabbit grabbed his paw. "It's quite safe," she said. "A party is a Truce. He's quite friendly here, although he won't recognise you when he meets you out late. You mustn't go. We will start without him."

"We are going to begin with 'Blind Man's Buff,'" said Squirrel, "so that you will all feel at home. Come along, Hedgehog, and be blindfolded."

Amidst much laughter, she tied the handkerchief over Hedgehog's eyes, twisted him three times round, and then sprang away. Hedgehog groped about the room, catching his prickles in Grey Rabbit's cuffs, tearing Squirrel's dress, sticking a spike into Water Rat's frills, until at last he caught someone.

He pushed his hands over the face and ears of a little squirrel, but guessed wrong, and had to hunt again. Next he got Hare by the leg, and as Hare was by far the tallest in the room, it wasn't difficult to know who it was.

Hare, with a bandage over his eyes, leapt about the room, making the rabbits and squirrels scuttle with screams of delight.

Mole sat quietly in a corner, with Hare groping over him, until suddenly, as he tried to slip through Hare's legs, he was caught.

"I'm half-blind already," said he. "I don't need a handkerchief," but Squirrel tied him up like the others. Straightway he caught Grey Rabbit, and she pounced on the youngest rabbit, who ran up and down like a clockwork toy.

There was a little sobbing noise under the table, and Grey Rabbit turned up the cloth to see if a mouse or a frog were hiding there. Fuzzypeg, the young Hedgehog, sat weeping into his new spotted handkerchief.

"Nobody's found me!" he wailed. "I'm nobody's nuffin!" So Grey Rabbit and Squirrel lifted him out, and comforted him, and helped him to be found.

They all sat down to tea, tightly squeezed against each other in the little room, and Squirrel, Hare, and little Grey Rabbit filled the plates and mugs as soon as they were empty. Like snow in summer the iced cake and buns disappeared, and the barley loaves and oat cakes and sandwiches faded away before the hungry small animals, who had never seen such a feast.

"Wise Owl has forgotten to come," said Hare, happily, as he passed the mince-pies, and gobbled some on the way.

Grey Rabbit set aside a portion for her chief guest, lest he should be tempted by the smallest rabbit to forget the Truce.

Hare cut the big cake and gave every one his portion, with a piece of the cold snow and ice from the top. They smacked their lips, and said, "Yes, please," when Hare offered a second helping.

" 'Turn the Trencher' next!" shouted Hare, jumping up from the table, as soon as he had finished, and little Fuzzypeg and the youngest rabbits hastily stuffed their

pieces of cake in their pockets and jumped up with the rest.

They pushed the table back, and all sat in a circle on the floor. Then Hare spun the silvery-white coin, and round and round it went like a humming top.

"Fuzzypeg," called he, and the little Hedgehog rushed out and caught it before it fell.

"Little Grey Rabbit," called Fuzzypeg, but Grey Rabbit could not get there in time, and the trencher fell.

"A Forfeit," shouted Hare, and Grey Rabbit gave him her white cuff. Then she turned the trencher and called, "Mole." Mole was so slow, he, too, had to pay a forfeit – a button off his velvet waistcoat. When Hare had a collection of forfeits, he stopped the game and crouched on the ground with his face hidden in his paws.

"Here is a thing, and a very pretty thing. What is the owner of this pretty thing to do?" asked Grey Rabbit, holding a red scarf over his head.

"You must cry in one corner, laugh in another, dance in another, and sing in another," said Hare, triumphantly getting his jingle right. Poor old Hedgehog caused much laughter by weeping, and guffawing, and dancing, and then singing in a husky voice a ditty called, "The lass that loved a milkman."

The next forfeit was Squirrel's, and she went through the same performance, dancing lightly on her small toes, laughing in her dainty way, crying in a tiny whimper, and singing very sweetly, "Here we go gathering Nuts in May," when the door was pushed open, and Wise Owl stalked in.

"Sorry I'm late," said he. "I was detained hunting." But every one had disappeared in a twinkling, under the table, behind the chairs, and even in the grandfather clock. Only little Grey Rabbit remained to receive him.

"Where's the party?" he asked. "Come out! Don't be afraid!"

One by one the animals crawled out, looking rather sheepish, and the game continued, with Wise Owl applauding solemnly in the arm-chair, as he ate his tea, until all the forfeits were redeemed.

"Now play 'Hunt the Thimble,'" said Grey Rabbit, and she brought out her tiny silver thimble with roses round the edge.

"You hide it first, Wise Owl," said she, bowing to him, and they all bundled out of the room into the garden, where they stood whispering and staring at the bright stars, and the great moon.

Owl looked here, and he looked there. He looked up at the ceiling, and down at the floor, but he could not see a good place. He took the thimble in his beak, and swallowed it.

Then he called the others in, and of course they couldn't find it anywhere at all.

"We give it up," said they in chorus.

"I've swallowed it," said Wise Owl, and nobody dared to laugh. Little Grey Rabbit nearly cried.

"But – but – I can't do my mending now," she faltered.

"But – but – we can't play now," cried Squirrel.

"We'll hide something else. The trencher will do," said Owl.

"Don't swallow that," said Mole boldly. "It's my breastplate, which I found in the ploughfield one day when the men had been ploughing." Again they all trooped outside, and Owl put his great clawed feathery foot over the trencher.

"Come in," he called. "Now find it." They hunted, and then Fuzzypeg saw it gleaming between Owl's toes.

He whispered to the smallest rabbit and she told another, who told another, till at last the rumour reached Grey Rabbit.

"Under your toes," said she, "and Fuzzypeg found it."

"It wasn't found because it wasn't lost," said Wise Owl, and Hare murmured, "Lost in one corner, found in another, hidden in another, and swallowed in another."

"I must go now," said Wise Owl. "I have another engagement a few miles away." He stared at all the company with his great unwinking eyes, and then waddled to the door.

"Thank you, Grey Rabbit, for a very pleasant evening," said he, bowing, and he turned and flew up into the sky.

Hare mopped his brow, and all the small animals jumped for joy.

"Let us end up with a dance," said Water Rat, who had been very quiet all evening, for he did not wish Wise Owl to notice him. So they danced the polka, and Hare played the jolly little tune on his flute. Grey Rabbit hopped round with Mole, Squirrel with Water Rat, and the Hedgehogs turned by themselves, for they were too prickly to clasp one another. All the little brown rabbits and the squirrels pirouetted and jigged, but no one danced as prettily as little Grey Rabbit, in her silver birch shoes.

Then someone looked out at the moon, which was sailing high in the sky. There was the Great Bear, waiting up above, and the gold star, Sirius, which every little animal knows, was beaming down to light them home.

"Good-night! Good-night!" they said, as they wrapped their mufflers round their necks and took each other's arms. "Thank you, Squirrel, Hare, and Grey Rabbit for the most beautiful party."

They all carried beech-nut boxes of sugar, and Hedgehog took the walnut shells of honey to leave at the little round doors of the cottages where field-mice live.

Hare put his flute in its case, and Squirrel and Grey Rabbit tidied away the crumbs from the feast. Then upstairs they all went to bed, yawning sleepily.

Little Grey Rabbit folded her scarf of cobweb, and laid it in a drawer. She stuffed her silver-birch slippers with sheeps' wool, and put them away. Then she opened her attic window and held her blue beads up in the moonlight, so that they shone like blue flames.

"Although I did lose my dear thimble, it was a most beautiful party," she whispered, but only the bare trees and the twinkling stars heard her.

The End of the Story

Wise Owl's Story

Wise Owl lived in the hollow oak tree in the middle of the wood. Anyone could see it was Wise Owl's house, for a little silver bell with an eagle on it, and curly lines like a shell round its edges, hung beside the front door. There were windows high up in the tree, hidden in the rough bark, and a wisp of blue smoke came out of the chimney among the leaves, when Owl was at home.

The house was very old and very untidy. Dust and dirt of ages filled the rooms, and cobwebs hung in festoons from the ceilings. Sometimes bits of tree fell into the soup when Wise Owl was cooking, but he was too wise a bird to mind, and he stirred them about with his wooden spoon, murmuring, "How interesting!"

"A morsel of a house which has lasted since Queen Elizabeth's time gives a tasty flavour to the broth!"

There were little attics and storerooms all over the

tree, filled with lumber and old wood, and spiders. Wise Owl never went into these rooms, for he kept to his kitchen, his bedroom, and his study.

In the bedroom there was a little four-poster, with a small carved owl perched on each bed-post, and on it lay a goose-feather bed. In the kitchen was a frying-pan, but in the study were all Owl's books of wisdom. Round the walls were shelves, and there the books were arranged, books in green, brown, and beautiful red bindings, exactly the same colours as the leaves of the trees.

The books of poetry and rhyme were green, like the young leaves of spring.

Those on history and arithmetic were brown, like the dead leaves of winter, and the story books were *red* (which is an Owlish joke). Owl had always loved reading, ever since he was a small Owlet, and had peered, one moonlight night, through the window of a museum. He had seen, in a glass case, a Greek coin with an owl upon it, and he knew he was a bird of wisdom.

One evening, just as dusk fell, Owl yawned and got down from his easy-chair, where he had been dozing. He sniffed at the cool air which came through the window. The wind had changed, and there was a strange rippling motion which he felt at once in his feathers.

"A storm's brewing somewhere," said he to himself. "There will be a gale to-night. I must shut the windows before I go out, or my books will get wet."

He took down his weather book, and turned the pages, which fluttered in the breeze like the leaves in the trees around. He sat down in the doorway and read some wisdom about cyclones and rain-drops, and he nodded his wise old head as he read.

Then he took a sip of little Grey Rabbit's primrose wine, and watched the moon sail in the night sky among great ragged black clouds. The clouds came hurrying up, whipped by the rising wind, the Wise Owl flew off over the woods and fields. He had to go far that night before he found his supper.

The wind whirled through the wood in a fury. It tossed the trees and snapped the branches. It rattled and banged at the doors and windows of all the little houses in the fields and hedgerows. It screamed through the key-holes, and whistled down the chimneys, and shook the tiny doors.

Mole, in his underground house, knew nothing of the storm. He lay underneath his blanket, dreaming of music and songs, but Mrs Hedgehog awoke her husband in the cottage close by.

"There's a crash!" said she. "Get up, Hedgehog, and see what's the matter. I believe our house has blown down."

Old Hedgehog crawled sleepily to the window, and stared out. On the ground under the hedge was a little hollow chimney, rolling about among the leaves.

"Th' chimbley's come off," said he. "It was a great

noise for our little chimbley."

"What shall we do? Suppose the house blows away?" cried Mrs Hedgehog, clutching the bedside.

"Our house is safe enough, wife," answered Hedgehog. "It's the big things that goes in a storm. Church steeples, and great trees, not tiddley houses like ours, close to the ground. That chimbley would never have been blowed off if it hadn't been stuck up. A good riddance!" He climbed back to bed and fell asleep in spite of Mrs Hedgehog's protests.

The sound of the wind and the echo of a crash awoke Hare, in the little house at the end of the wood.

"My goodness! It will blow my whiskers off," he cried, and he pulled the bedclothes over his long ears.

Squirrel shivered and curled her tail closely round her shoulders. Little Grey Rabbit in her attic opened her eyes, and listened to the creaking of the trees in the wood. After a time she heard a strange wailing voice which seemed to come from somewhere near.

"Too-whit, too-whoo! I've lost my ho-o-ome!" moaned through the night air, but when she sat up in bed she heard nothing except the screech of the wind. "I was dreaming," said she.

When Wise Owl's hunting was over, he tried to fly back to his tree, but the wind blew him out of his path, and he was very tired with buffeting against the blast. He knew the wood so well he could find his way home blindfolded, so, with his eyes half-shut, he blundered on

towards his front door.

But it wasn't there! He gasped with surprise, and circled round, but there was no silver bell, no little brown door, no great oak tree!

"Am I bewitched?" said he. "Have I come to the wrong wood?" He flew among the tree-tops and found the familiar outlines, the plumes and tufts and spires of the trees he knew. Then he looked down to the ground, and he saw the oak tree stretched there like a fallen giant. The door was broken off, books lay scattered on the grass, a dictionary floated like a white lily on a pool of rain-water, and the silver bell had gone.

"Oh woe! Woe is me!" cried the Owl. "Too-Whit! Too-Whoo! What shall I do?" His great wisdom deserted him, and he was just a lonely unhappy owl, very wet and very tired, with no home to rest in.

The wind screamed with glee, and tossed his books about, wetting the tiny pages, blowing them about like dandelion clocks. The trees swished him with their wet branches, lashed him with stinging whips, and he had no shelter. He rose up and flapped his way over the wood, and it was then that little Grey Rabbit heard his plaintive cry.

The next morning the gale dropped, but the rain poured down. The little rabbit could hear the patter of the drops on the roof as she dressed, and she looked from her window at a drenched world.

"I wonder what that crash was I heard in the night,"

said she to herself. "I'll just slip out while the others are asleep. I want to wear my new goloshes."

She brought out her shiny goloshes from the hole under the stairs. She bent them backwards and forwards like willow saplings, and sniffed at the nice smell.

Where did they come from? Nobody knew. They appeared on the doorstep one morning, with "A Present for Grey Rabbit" written on a holly leaf, but Mole and Hedgehog had never even heard of them. The strange thing was that it had never rained since they came, so little Grey Rabbit was glad to wear them. She slipped a cloak over her shoulders and ran out in the wet, down the path to the wood.

"My feet are quite dry!" she exclaimed, as she paddled through a pool, and she paddled back again, just to feel like a duck.

When she got near Wise Owl's house, she saw the fallen tree and the broken door and all the tumbled wet books.

"Oh! Poor Wise Owl! What will he do with no home!" she cried, and she gathered up some of the books, and put them under the tree for shelter.

She looked round for Wise Owl, but he was nowhere to be seen, so she hurried back with her sad news.

"We must all do something," said Hare, as he ate his porridge.

"Yes, let's do something really useful," said Squirrel, and she sipped daintily at her tea.

"Should we invite him here as our guest till he finds another house?" asked Grey Rabbit.

"Here?" exclaimed Hare, puckering up his face. "In this house, Grey Rabbit? Are you mad?"

"He'd break our cups with his wings," said Squirrel. "He'd be asleep all day, when we wanted to tidy the house, and make the beds. Besides, his ways are not our ways." She shivered.

"No, it wouldn't do," agreed Grey Rabbit. "He must have a house of his own. The little birds will mob him if they see him. It isn't right for a respectable old wise-acre like Owl to be pecked and teased by jeering common sparrows and jays."

"He must have a nice big house to hold all those books of wisdom which I saw lying in the rain."

There was silence for a moment, and then Grey Rabbit said, "Suppose we go out and look for one for him."

"Can't he do that himself?" grumbled Squirrel.

"He doesn't like the daylight, you know, and at night he is too busy," said Grey Rabbit. "We will wait till the rain stops, and then we will take sandwiches and spend the day house-hunting."

"Sandwiches? Splendid!" cried Hare. "I love house-hunting!" He ran to the door and looked out.

"There's a rainbow in the sky, Grey Rabbit. We can go quite soon."

The three animals set out on their expedition through the wood, but although they looked to the right and the

left, high up and low down, they couldn't find a hollow tree.

Squirrel jumped among the tree-tops, and Hare leaped high on the ground, and little Grey Rabbit ran with her nose in the air, sniffing and hunting, but there didn't seem to be a house to spare anywhere.

They took their sandwiches out of their pockets and sat down to eat them near the fallen tree. Grey Rabbit fished the little dictionary out of the pool, and wiped it on her handkerchief. Squirrel found a book of nursery songs in a briar bush. Hare picked up a history book, but that was quite dry.

"I wonder where Wise Owl is," said Grey Rabbit, and she peeped through the door into the dusty rooms. "I hope he hasn't flown away to another country."

"He's somewhere about," said Hare placidly. "I don't want to see him."

"He is as dull as this history book." He flung it into the pond, where it lay, still dry.

"Let us all go different ways," said Squirrel. "Then if we haven't found a house by tea-time, we will go home."

"And have plum cake for tea," sighed Hare hungrily.

"And hot buttered toast," said Squirrel.

Hare tossed a straw in the air, to see which way he should go, and then he set off down an inviting little green path.

He soon found himself out of the wood, in a wet green

meadow. There in the grass grew round, white satiny knobs.

"Mushrooms!" he cried, and he filled his pockets. He forgot all about Wise Owl's house as he wandered about the field. At the gate he met an elderly rabbit, leaning on a crutch, and they stood talking of the storm.

"Such a wind! It blew the garden gate off its hinges," said the rabbit, "and I hobbled in for my breakfast. I haven't had such a feast since my accident. 'It's an ill wind that blows nobody good,' as my father used to say."

"Is the gate still down?" asked Hare.

"Oh yes. There's plenty left," replied the rabbit. Hare thanked him, gave him a pawful of mushrooms, and then ran with his long legs across the fields to the farm garden.

Squirrel started off along a little path in the opposite direction, but soon she saw a hazel tree with round brown nuts clustering upon it. She sprang up the boughs, and feasted, cracking the shells and nibbling the sweet kernels.

"Ah! Why can't I come here every day?" she asked herself. She went a little farther and came to a mountain ash.

Up she ran, and rubbed her cheeks against the scarlet berries. She picked a bunch, and threaded them on a grass. Then she hung them round her neck, and gazed at herself in a pool of rainwater.

"Scarlet suits me," said she, simpering, and she

certainly looked very pretty with her necklace.

A silver birch stood in her path, and she stood before the lovely white tree, with its tiny pointed leaves. She stripped off a piece of the bark, and wound it round her paws.

"Grey Rabbit's slippers are made of silver birch, those the Toad sent to her," she mused. She tried to weave a pair for her own tiny feet, but it was more difficult than she supposed, and she flung the silken strips away.

Then she ran up the tree and sported herself on the delicate sprays of green.

"It's like a roundabout at the fair," said she, swinging to and fro. "Lulla-lullaby," she sang, and she rocked herself up and down till the tree shook with her antics.

Then she curled up in a corner and went to sleep, for the leaves were fragrant, and the branch was soft. She forgot all about Wise Owl and his home, as she lay curled up high in the air. When she awoke it was too late to bother, and she gaily danced her way home.

Little Grey Rabbit ran along the path to the West, looking to right and left for a hollow tree. She dodged in and out, sniffing and searching, and she marked each tree with a tiny white cross, so that none should be overlooked.

She worked so hard she did not notice that the afternoon had passed and evening was approaching. She tapped the trees, and marked them, moving farther and farther from home, until at last she heard the sound

she had been listening for all day.

She stopped in front of a great beech tree and tapped again. It was hollow!

Here was a house for Wise Owl! She ran round the trunk and pulled away the brambles and leaves which concealed the opening. Then, rather frightened, she went inside.

There was a splendid empty house! It was rather damp, of course, but a little fire would soon dry it. There were three rooms, and lots of attics, and shelves all round the walls. It was just right for Wise Owl.

She went to the door and looked out.

The moon was rising behind the hill, and a soft golden glow spread over the wood. A moonbeam shone into the doorway, and lighted up a pool of water on the ground.

Grey Rabbit thought of Wise Owl just starting on his rounds, and she felt frightened. She thought of her home, and the supper table, and bright fire, the ticking clock, and the cosy hearth, and she felt very lonely. She didn't know where she was, and there was nothing to be done, except to stay there all night.

She picked up a tiny glow-worm and carried it in with her. Then she pulled some wood across the door-way, to keep out foxes, and stoats, and savage beasts, which might roam through the wood at night.

She climbed on to a rough shelf, made herself as small as possible, and fell asleep, with the glow-worm shining like a little night-light.

When Hare had eaten half the lettuce bed he went home, and there he found Squirrel who sat with her necklace round her neck, rocking herself backwards and forwards, and reading one of Owl's books.

"I got here first," she said. "I won the prize."

"What prize?" asked Hare.

"The prize for getting here first. The mushrooms," said she.

"How did you know?" asked the bewildered Hare, emptying his pockets.

"By the knobs in your coat," said Squirrel calmly.

"Where is little Grey Rabbit?" asked Hare. "Hasn't she come home yet?"

"No, she probably met Wise Owl, and they talked about tails and bells, and hollow trees," said Squirrel. "She'll come soon."

They had tea without her, but when supper-time came, and there was no little Grey Rabbit, they both grew anxious.

Hare put a lighted candle in the window to light her home, and then he stood at the door and called, "Coo-ee. Coo-ee. Coo-ee." His voice rang through the air, but there was no answer.

"Coo-ee. Coo-ee." he called again, and "Too-Whit, Too-Whoo," a shrill voice hooted nearby.

Hare started. Who was that? Where did that noise come from?

Wise Owl came out of the woodshed, yawning with

49

wide open mouth.

"Did you call?" he asked coolly.

"We've lost Grey Rabbit," explained Hare nervously.

"What is she doing out late like this?" asked the Owl.

"She is looking for a house for you."

"A house for me?" echoed Wise Owl. "I am going to live in your wood-shed. It is warm and comfortable, and there is plenty of food about."

He stepped into the house and snapped up all the mushrooms and hot buttered toast which lay ready for supper.

Squirrel dived under a chair and lay there shaking with fright. Hare fidgeted on one leg, and said nothing.

"I'd better go off and find Grey Rabbit," said Wise Owl. "You stay here, and wait up for her. You'd be lost if you came too." He flew off with his ghost-like flight, a silently moving shadow, and Hare mopped his brow.

"Whew!" he cried. "I did feel nervous. I never thought I should live to see the day when an Owl would come into the kitchen and eat my supper before my very eyes!"

"Better to eat your supper, than to eat you," said Squirrel, crawling from under the chair. "He's been eating the mice in the wood-shed all day, or he might have gobbled you, Hare."

"Stuff and nonsense," said Hare, and he sat down to wait for the Owl's return.

Wise Owl flew over the woods, calling, but either the

tree was too thick or Grey Rabbit was too fast asleep, she never heard his voice, and he had to return without her.

"She's lost!" he said huskily. "Little Grey Rabbit's gone. I asked Rat, who thumped along the hedge-side with that knot in his tail, but he hadn't seen her. I asked the stoat, and several other night people, but no one had seen her."

Hare and Squirrel were very much alarmed, for Wise Owl was a famous finder of lost animals.

"I am going to sleep now," said he. "Don't disturb me. You two must go out and look for her. The morning's here, and Hedgehog the milkman is starting his rounds. I saw him trying to put a broken chimney on his roof. I ordered an extra jug of milk for myself."

"Now hurry up," commanded the Owl, as he stood in the doorway. "No dilly-dallying! No shilly-shallying! Turn up your sleeves, Hare, and take that necklace from your neck, Squirrel. Off you go to look for your companion!"

The two animals sprang up, and got ready, with sticks and map and compass, and Owl returned to the wood-shed.

"He orders us about as if he lived here," complained Squirrel. "Oh, I do wish Grey Rabbit would come back!"

There was a sound outside, the door was pushed open, and in came little Grey Rabbit, looking as fresh as a daisy. She had washed in a stream, and brushed her hair with a teasel brush.

"Wherever have you been?" cried Hare. "We were just going to look for you. Owl was hunting for you all night."

Little Grey Rabbit turned pale.

"To find you, not to eat you," said Hare crossly. "We never went to bed, and here you are looking as if you had been enjoying yourself."

"I am so sorry," said Grey Rabbit humbly. "I got lost. I must have walked in a circle, for I was really quite near Owl's old tree, and I didn't know. I found a home for Owl!"

"Thank goodness," exclaimed Hare, and he flung himself on the rocking chair with relief. Then he hesitated.

"Is it a nice house, Grey Rabbit? Owl is in the wood-shed, and he won't go away unless it is a nicer house than ours."

"Couldn't we spring-clean it for him, whilst he is asleep, and put his books inside, and then he will want to go?" asked Squirrel.

"Oh yes," cried Grey Rabbit, who loved to polish and scrub. "But I am so hungry.

"I had nothing to eat last night, and this morning there wasn't time to stop."

"Owl ate our supper last night," said Hare gloomily, "but luckily he didn't notice the larder door."

Squirrel hustled round, and soon a plate of porridge

and treacle was ready for the rabbit.

They then took buckets and mops and scrubbing brushes and soap, and walked off to the wood.

Grey Rabbit led them to a beautiful beech tree, with golden brown leaves spreading in a tent overhead, and thousands of beech-nuts hanging from the branches, and spilling on the warm earth.

"I shouldn't mind living here myself," said Squirrel as she cracked the three-cornered nuts and ate the tiny kernels. "We will take some of these home for beech-bread."

"It's a fine tree," said Hare, "but where is the door?" Grey Rabbit pointed out the small hole near the ground.

"Owl won't want to fly down to the earth when he comes home," objected Hare. "I don't think he will change from the wood-shed."

Then he added hurriedly, "Excuse me a moment. I've forgotten something. I must run home," and away he went.

"He doesn't want to scrub and rub," said Squirrel crossly, but Grey Rabbit took her into the tree, and she forgot her disapproval of Hare as she explored the rooms.

"It's a very nice house," said she, "fit for a king."

They filled their buckets from the pool near-by, and they scrubbed and mopped the floors and walls and ceilings. They washed the little shelves and book-cases, and the cupboards which hung all round the tree.

"I do like plenty of cupboards," sighed Grey Rabbit

54

happily, as she fastened a knob on the door.

They beeswaxed the shelves, and lined them with fresh beech-leaves, and they hung a bunch of wild thyme on a wooden nail to make a sweet smell.

"Owl will be able to keep all his books here," said Squirrel and she put some pointed chestnut leaves on the floor for green carpets. "There's a place for his blotting-paper, and his pen and ink, and——"

"Tape measure and thimble," interrupted a voice, and Hare came in carrying a saw.

"What's that for?" asked Squirrel.

"It's a saw to saw things," said Hare. "You never thought, but I did."

He sat down on a bench and folded his arms.

"Do you imagine that Wise Owl would live here with that door? Why he couldn't get through it without crawling! I could scarcely get my ears inside, and he would have to leave his wings in the wood!" Hare laughed and went on, "I said to myself, 'That Owl will want to live in our wood-shed if we don't do something.' So I'm going to make a door, high up, so that he can fly right in, and no burglars can get to his rooms."

He climbed up the steep stairs, and cut a neat door in the tree.

He fastened hinges of springy bark, so that no one would notice it. Then he cut a window in Owl's study, which was very dark and dismal, and put another in the kitchen.

"A nice airy house with every modern convenience," said he proudly, as he stepped backwards to view his work, but he trod on the soap and fell downstairs to the bottom of the tree.

"The proper place to keep soap is the larder, so put it there," cried he, rubbing his head, and calling up to Squirrel. "Never leave soap on the stairs, Squirrel." So Squirrel placed it on the larder shelf.

The three animals went to the oak tree and collected the books, which were now dry with the wind and the sun.

They carried them across to the new house, and arranged them on the shelves. They picked up Owl's cuckoo clock which hung in a bush. "Cuckoo! Cuckoo! Cuckoo!" it struck.

"Is this one of Owl's magics?" cried Squirrel. "I wondered why the first cuckoo was always heard in this wood!" They hung it on the staircase, and returned for Owl's rush-bottomed chair, and three-legged stool, his feather-bed and frying-pan. Hare found the sealing-wax, and Squirrel the candlestick, and little Grey Rabbit found Owl's night-cap dangling in the nettles, but nowhere could they see the little silver bell.

"Moley's bell," sighed little Grey Rabbit. "It was such a beautiful bell, and it saved my tail. I do hope it will turn up."

They all hunted round the wood for house-warming presents for the Owl, to welcome him when he came to his new home. Hare picked a robin's red pin-cushion, to hold Owl's needles and pins. Squirrel got a piece of honeycomb from a wild bees' nest. Little Grey Rabbit gathered some starry moss, for a green cushion.

The house was finished and they stood in the grass staring up and admiring the shiny grey trunk of the tree, and the sloping boughs with the little door hidden among them, when Hedgehog walked up.

"Hello!" said he. "I've just found Owl's bell. I was walking along the path through the wood, looking for a new chimbley for our house, when I heard a tinkly tinkle, and there was a mouse playing with Owl's bell! Did you ever hear the like? A mouse with Owl's bell!"

"A bold mouse!" said Hare. "Luckily for him, Owl is asleep in our wood-shed."

He explained the disasters of the night of the storm.

Hedgehog nodded. "Just what I told my Missus," said he. "Great oaks fall and little acorns weather the gale."

Little Grey Rabbit took the silver bell and examined it. It was none the worse but she rubbed it, and polished it.

Then Squirrel ran up the tree and hung it at the side of Owl's front door, and the four walked back to the little house at the edge of the wood.

"Wake up, Wise Owl," they cried, tapping on his door. "Wake up. There's a new house for you in the wood."

"Don't want a new house," muttered Wise Owl

sleepily. "Go away and play."

"Your books are on the shelves," said Hare.

"Your cuckoo clock's ticking on the stairs," said Squirrel.

"Your night-cap is on the bed," said Grey Rabbit.

"Your bell's a-tinkling by the front door," said Hedgehog.

Wise Owl came out and blinked at them.

"Did you say you had put my tree up again?" he asked.

"No. We've found another, a better one," said little Grey Rabbit.

Without another word Wise Owl flew off, flapping silently away in the daylight, never heeding the crowd of small birds which followed after. They twittered and cried, but Owl saw the silver bell, and he pushed open the door. He walked upstairs, one step at a time, and he looked in all the cupboards and on the shelves. He counted his books, and only one was missing – the nursery songs which Squirrel had taken home with her, but Owl knew those ditties by heart.

He threw open the round window which Hare had made, and looked at the great roof of the tree above him. He ran his beak over the smooth floor, and smelled the sweet sawdust which lay in a pile on the floor.

"A pinch of a house that was here in King Charles's time gives a sharp relish to the broth," said he, and he carried the little heap to the larder, ready for his soup-making. Then he saw the delicate honeycomb and the cake of soap.

"The honey I'll keep for to-morrow, but this cake will do for my supper before I go hunting."

He swallowed it, and snapped his beak.

"Tasty! A tasty morsel!" said he. "That was somebody's kind thought! I must give a present each to the Squirrel, the Hare and the little Grey Rabbit. They've certainly done me a good turn. Something for something has always been Owl's motto."

He searched in his treasure box, which was buried deep in the brown leaf-mould of the wood, and he took them – what do you think?

A tiny basket, carved out of a cherry stone; a sailing boat, made from half a walnut-shell; a little beech-tree growing out of a beech-nut! Now can you guess which had which?

The End of the Story

Little Grey Rabbit's Washing Day

It was a lovely April morning, and the sky was blue as a speedwell flower. Across it moved white clouds like little boats sailing to the west.

A fresh wind was behind them, and it caught the hazel trees, too, and fluttered their catkins.

Grey Rabbit stood at the window. The curtain flapped against her face, and the trees nodded their heads to her. She bobbed to them in return.

"Good morning, trees," said she. "I hope you are well." But the trees didn't answer. They only tossed their branches and shook their thousand yellow tails, so that the golden pollen flew in a shower.

There was a thump and a bump and Hare came bounding into the room.

"Grey Rabbit!" he called. "What are you staring at?"

"The nut trees, waving in the wind, and the little

63

clouds sailing over the blue sky," said Grey Rabbit.

"Oh!" said Hare, disappointed. "I thought you saw something nice to eat, or something to do, or something to play with, Grey Rabbit."

"I do. I see them all," laughed Grey Rabbit. "There are little spring cabbages growing under the hedges for you to eat, Hare. There are quick-moving shadows for you to play with, and if you want something to do, you can make a pair of slippers from the silver-birch skin, for it is peeling off ready for slipper-making."

"I don't want to do any of those things, Grey Rabbit," began Hare, and he stopped, for there was the sound of singing in the lane.

They could hear the words clearly, and this is the song they heard:

> "The gipsy walks the long road,
>   Her basket on her head.
> Her house is in the woodland,
>   The bracken is her bed."

"Who is it?" whispered Hare. "Who can it be?"

"She has a nice voice, whoever she is," said Grey Rabbit.

There was a click of the garden gate. Somebody was coming up the path.

It was a gipsy rabbit, with a green rush basket perched on her head. Round her neck was a coloured shawl.

She was very brown, and her hair was rough and tousled, with thorns and leaves sticking in it. Her eyes were bright as stars, and she came up to the door singing her song:

"Come buy my shining clothes-pegs,
     With bands of silver bound,
And peg your little apron
     In orchard drying-ground."

Hare and Grey Rabbit ran to the door and waited. Squirrel came leaping from the apple tree when she heard the gipsy's song.

The brown gipsy put her basket on the doorstep and nodded and smiled.

"Kind Grey Rabbit!" said she. "You'll buy my clothes-pegs, won't you?"

She stooped to the basket, and held up the neat roll of pegs, ivory white, with little silver bands round their waists. They were threaded together like a row of small dolls.

"Oh, how lovely!" cried Grey Rabbit. "I've always wanted some clothes-pegs to keep my washing from blowing away. I had some once, but they were not pretty like these. The rooks stole them and carried them off to make their nests. Now we can't keep the washing except by putting stones on it."

"Yes," added Squirrel eagerly. "The clothes blew up

65

in the trees last week, when there was a gale, and I had to climb among the boughs to bring them down."

"And another time I had to run a mile to catch a handkerchief. Away it flew, over the garden, across the brook, into the fields, and I had to run like the wind to catch it." Hare spoke breathlessly and the gipsy smiled at him.

"You can run fast, I warrant, Mister Hare."

"I should just think I can," boasted Hare. "I raced the wind itself that day and snatched my handkerchief out of its claws and carried it back. But it ruffled my fur and blew hard enough to take my whiskers off !"

"Will these clothes-pegs keep the things fast on the line?" asked Grey Rabbit.

"Yes, indeed, Grey Rabbit," said the gipsy. "I've sold my little pegs to many families, all over the world, and I have had many a letter thanking me."

She dived in her pocket and brought out a bundle of leaves. Even as she sorted them – holly leaves, beech leaves, oak leaves, in her brown paws – a gust of wind seized them and tossed them away.

"Oh dear!" cried Grey Rabbit. "All your letters gone."

"Plenty more," said the gipsy calmly. "Plenty more where these came from," and she pointed to the great woods. "Thousands and thousands of letters all thanking me," she said.

"It would be nice to have some real clothes-pegs,"

mused Grey Rabbit, and Squirrel and Hare nodded.

"These clothes-pegs will keep your little collar and cuffs and your blue apron on the line when the wind blows, Grey Rabbit. You never need fear they will go."

"They are beautiful little pegs," said Grey Rabbit, touching them gently. "Did you make them, Gipsy?"

"Yes. With my own paws I made them. The wood is holly with the green bark stripped away. The little girdles are made of silver from a silver mine I know."

"Oh!" said Hare, goggling his round eyes. "Oh!"

"I trimmed the pegs with my sharp knife," continued the gipsy, bringing a horn-handled knife from her pocket, and showing them the sharp blade. "Then I made little pointed ends, and bound two pieces together with the silver band to make a peg."

"Then I will buy your little clothes-pegs," said Grey Rabbit, and she clapped her paws for joy as she looked at them.

Squirrel was leaning over the gipsy's basket on the ground.

There were many bright things which attracted her, and she picked up first one and then another.

"Here is a brush to brush my tail," said she. "I should like this."

"We've got a teasel brush," Grey Rabbit reminded her.

"Here's a tin saucepan," said Squirrel.

"We've got a good saucepan," said Hare indignantly.

"But it's sticky since you made the toffee in it, Hare," objected Squirrel.

"That only adds a sweet flavour to the soup," said Hare.

"Well, here's a hand-glass," said Squirrel, holding up a tiny mirror.

"We don't need one," said Grey Rabbit quickly. "There's the stream at the bottom of the garden where you can see yourself."

"And there's a pond in the field," added Hare. "Don't be silly, Squirrel."

The gipsy smiled at Squirrel, and the little animal dived with her paws under the shining objects which filled the basket.

"Here's something," said she. "Here's something. What is it for? I'm sure we want it."

"It's a nutmeg grater," said the gipsy. "Here's the grater, all rough like a hedgehog's back. And here's the little box to keep the nutmeg in."

Squirrel squeaked with excitement and opened the little tin box.

"Oh! What is inside? A nut?" she cried.

"A nutmeg!" said the gipsy. "It's a rare thing, a nutmeg. It comes from over the sea. It doesn't grow on our trees in the woods."

"No," said Hare. "It doesn't grow on a hazel tree like the cobnuts, or on a walnut tree, like the walnuts, or on a chestnut tree like the chestnuts. It grows on a nutmeg tree!"

They were much impressed by Hare's knowledge, and they passed the nutmeg from one to another, and smelled it and licked it.

"What is it for?" asked Grey Rabbit.

"You rub it on the grater and sprinkle it in your cakes," said the gipsy.

"Oh, do buy the nutmeg grater, Grey Rabbit," shouted Hare.

"Yes, dear Grey Rabbit," said Squirrel, and Grey Rabbit agreed.

Then the gipsy sang another verse of her song and this is what she sang:

"I bought the wooden clothes-pegs,
   With their girdles of new tin,
I bought a little grater,
   To keep my nutmeg in."

"Tin?" cried Hare. "You said they were silver."

"Silver or tin, what's the difference?" asked the gipsy. "They both shine and that is all that matters."

"True," pondered Hare. "True. All is not gold that glitters, and all is not silver that shines. That is in Wise Owl's Book of Proverbs."

Grey Rabbit put her hand in her pocket and brought out an empty purse. She ran into the house and looked in the money-box.

There was nothing in it. She peeped in the tea-pot, and in the clock, for sometimes there was a penny or two hiding there. There was nothing at all.

"Oh dear!" she sighed. "What shall I do? I would like to have those clothes-pegs."

"Oh dear!" echoed Squirrel. "I do want the nutmeg grater."

Hare twiddled his thumbs and said nothing, for he hadn't a penny in the world.

Then Grey Rabbit spoke to the gipsy who was standing on the doorstep, smiling at the sky, smiling at the trees, caring nothing at all.

"I haven't any money. How shall I pay you?"

The gipsy looked at her with dark flashing eyes, and sang again:

> "I hadn't any money,
>   But the gipsy didn't care,
>   'Just a pair of ear-rings,
>   I'll take for 'em, my dear.'"

"Ear-rings?" cried Grey Rabbit and Squirrel.

Grey Rabbit whispered to Squirrel and Squirrel ran up the nut treee. She picked two little clusters of hazel catkins with their long greeny-yellow tails.

"Will these do?" asked Grey Rabbit, offering them to the gipsy.

"Just right," said the gipsy, and she fastened them to

her ears, and let them dangle like a pair of pretty tassels.

"Thank you, Grey Rabbit. Thank you, Squirrel and Hare. Blessings on your round faces," said the gipsy. "Good luck to your wash day."

"Thank you. Good luck to you, gipsy," called the three friends.

The gipsy swung her basket upon her head and curtsied low. Then away she went, with her skirt flapping and her ear-rings bobbing and her dark eyes sparkling.

She tripped down the garden path, and left Grey Rabbit holding the roll of wooden clothes-pegs and Squirrel the nutmeg grater.

Down the lane she went. They could just see her basket over the garden wall. They could hear her song, shrill and clear like a blackbird's whistle.

"Listen!" cried Hare, and this is what they heard:

> "I washed my little apron
>   And hung it up to dry.
>   The gipsy waved her hand to me,
>   And vanished in the sky."

"Goodness!" exclaimed Hare. "Did you hear what she said?"

He scampered to the gate, and saw the gipsy waving her brown arm. Then she slipped among the trees and disappeared.

"Perhaps she sailed away in one of those boats in the sky," said Grey Rabbit.

"Those aren't boats," said Hare scornfully. "They are clouds."

They stood for a while looking up into the sky, but nowhere could they see the gipsy rabbit. Then they returned to the house with their treasures.

Squirrel at once began to make a cake ready for the nutmeg. Grey Rabbit thought it would be a good plan to have a wash day. The sun was shining, and the little wind would dry the clothes.

She was longing to use her new bright clothes-pegs. She sent Hare across the common to ask if anybody wanted any clothes washed.

"Ask all our friends if they have any washing to be done. I'm going to have a big wash day, in honour of my silver-banded clothes-pegs," said she.

Hare nodded importantly, and galloped off. He knocked at every little cottage in the woods and lanes. He peeped in at open windows, and called to tree-houses:

"Any washing to-day? Grey Rabbit's wash day. Any washing to-day?"

Down came the little animals with small garments, cobweb scarves, sheep's wool blankets, tiny handkerchiefs, leafy towels. Some of them carried their bundles to Grey Rabbit's house. Some of them put their clothes in wheel-barrows and trundled them across the field.

Some scampered with trailing sheets and bits of

ribbon. And Hare ran on, knocking at doors, tapping at shutters, calling through key-holes.

"Any washing to-day for Grey Rabbit's wash-tub?"

He even went to Wise Owl and rang the bell. Wise Owl roused himself from his deep sleep and opened the door a crack.

"Go away! I don't want anything," he said crossly, when he saw Hare.

"Please, Wise Owl——" began Hare.

"Go away," grunted Wise Owl. "I don't want anything. I'm asleep." He shook his head violently and his nightcap fell off and floated down to Hare.

"Thank you, sir," said Hare, seizing it and running off.

"Go away," said Wise Owl sleepily, and he went back to bed. "Oh dear," he muttered. "I believe I dropped my nightcap. Well, I shall leave it now." He yawned and fell asleep again.

Mrs Hedgehog said that Fuzzypeg's smock was dirty, and she would be very glad if Grey Rabbit would wash it.

Moldy Warp asked Hare if Grey Rabbit would wash his best scarf. He had soiled it underground.

The Speckledy Hen sent her green sun-bonnet, and Mrs Rat gave Hare her apron with her compliments and thanks.

A couple of rabbits on the common brought their little frilled pinafores, and an old mother rabbit sent her sheep's-wool shawl. A mouse sent a handkerchief so small that it got lost on the way, and a butterfly sent a pair of bedroom slippers. A spider brought her silken web, and a fly his black suit.

A frog brought his green coat, and a dormouse sent her blanket. Everybody was glad little Grey Rabbit was going to have a real wash day, and there was a flutter of wings and a scutter of little feet bearing garments and fine clothes for the wash-tub.

Grey Rabbit put her own handkerchiefs and night-gown and blue apron in the wash, and Squirrel brought her yellow dress. Hare came hurrying home with a bundle of odds and ends of clothing.

He warmed the water, and carried it outside and poured it in a tub. Everything was ready, but there was no soap. High and low they hunted – under the table, in the wood-shed, in the teapot.

At last Grey Rabbit found it in the flour-bin, where Hare had left it on baking day.

Squirrel ran up the apple tree and tied the clothes line to a branch. Then she ran up the pear tree and fastened the other end. The rope hung in such a lovely loop she couldn't resist swinging on it. Hare pushed her gently backward and forward till it broke, and she had to tie it again.

Grey Rabbit stood at the wash-tub, which Hare had placed among the daisies. She rubbed and scrubbed and dipped each little garment, and soaped and rinsed them

77

till they were clean. Then she tossed them into the clothes-basket, and Hare and Squirrel carried them to the stream. They dabbled them in the clear water, and shook them, and threw them up in the air like balls.

"Now to hang them on the line," said Grey Rabbit, when they returned, laughing and swinging the basket. "Now for the little clothes-pegs."

She climbed on an upturned tub and pegged each article as Squirrel held it to her. There was a fine row of socks and handkerchiefs, of towels and smocks and frocks, hanging up to dry.

The wind came hurrying over the grass, and it tugged and pulled at the little garments, but the shining gipsy clothes-pegs held them firmly. So it blew into each one, and puffed it out as if it were alive. The clothes leaped and danced on the line; the little smocks filled out as if small fat bodies were inside them; the furry stockings looked as if they had a pair of legs.

The wind caught Fuzzypeg's smock and Squirrel's dress and little Grey Rabbit's apron, and Hare's pyjamas, and blew them as if stout animals were within.

The clothes-pegs held tightly to the line, the silver bands glittered, the rope swung, and all the clothes bobbed and curtsied. Little Grey Rabbit, who stood watching them, bobbed and curtsied back.

"There never was such a wash day in all the country-side as this," said she proudly to Squirrel and Hare.

Now somebody else was watching the row of washing,

dancing on the clothes line. The Fox crept out of the wood to see what all the fuss was about. He thought it was a party.

He saw Fuzzypeg's smock dangling there, and Squirrel's yellow dress, all puffed out, and he licked his lips.

"Fuzzypeg and Squirrel having a swing," said he. "Lots of people swinging! They look uncommonly fat! They must have eaten a big dinner! If I creep up very quietly, I may catch them and carry them home for tea."

He waited in the bushes, hiding under the brambles till Grey Rabbit went into the house.

Then he crept up very softly, and took a great spring. He grabbed Fuzzypeg's smock with one paw and Squirrel's yellow dress with another. But they wouldn't come down!

Whoo-oo-oo! whistled the wind.

Swish-swish-swish! went the clothes line.

Tinkle! Tinkle! Tinkle! rang the little clothes-pegs, and the Fox leapt back in alarm.

"Dear me!" he cried. "They are empty! There's nobody inside them! They are only wind-bags!"

And away he went, feeling very cross.

Next came a weasel. It wasn't the old Weasel, who was killed long ago, but his son, who was a traveller. He happened to be passing that way looking for something to eat, and he saw the row of washing, bobbing and dancing on the low line.

"Hallo! Fat little animals swinging on a rope! Having some fun! Just right for my tea!" said he. "I'll grab that stout little fellow in a blue smock."

He took a hop and a leap right over the garden bed, and he sprang on the back of the wind-filled smock which was Fuzzypeg's. But he clasped nothing at all!

Whoo-oo-oo, whistled the wind.

Swish-sh-sh, hissed the clothes line.

Tinkle-tinkle-tinkle, rang the little clothes-pegs, and the Weasel fell on the ground with a thump.

"Nothing in them! Empty clothes," he muttered, as he rubbed his bruised head. "I won't stay here where they play jokes. I shall go right away."

And off he went through the woods to another part of the world.

Next came old Hedgehog with his cans of milk.

"Hallo! What is young Fuzzypeg doing here, a-swinging on Grey Rabbit's clothes line?" he asked. "That young fellow ought to be at home! I'll catch him a whack!"

He crept softly up to the clothes line and grabbed the tail of the smock.

Tinkle, tinkle, tinkle, rang the little clothes-pegs.

"Dear me! It's not Fuzzypeg at all! It's only his smock filled with air. Dear me! How foolish I am! It must be Grey Rabbit's washing-day, as my Missis was telling me. But I've never seen clothes-pegs that called out to warn you, and I've never seen clothes so lifelike."

Grey Rabbit came running from the house. After her came Squirrel and Hare with the clothes-basket.

"Oh, Hedgehog! Did you hear some bells ringing?"

"Yes, Miss Grey Rabbit. Bells ring if you touch the washing-line. There's some magic in those clothes-pegs of yours. I was just taking hold of Fuzzypeg's smock, thinking that young fellow was hiding there, when the bells began to jingle. Wherever did you get such wonderful pegs?"

"I bought them from a gipsy, Hedgehog," said Grey Rabbit.

"Ah! That explains it. There's been a gipsy sleeping in the bracken, and she was making little clothes-pegs when I passed. Singing she was, and dancing in a fairy ring, and in her black pot was a brew of magical herbs. Yes, I saw her, but when I turned round she had gone – clean gone."

Grey Rabbit took down the dry clothes, and Hare and Squirrel folded them and laid them in the basket. Old Hedgehog watched admiringly, and he held the silvery clothes-pegs which Grey Rabbit handed to him.

"I got a nutmeg grater from the gipsy," said Squirrel. "Have you ever seen a nutmeg, Hedgehog?"

"I can't say as I have," said Hedgehog, cautiously.

"Here it is," said Squirrel, bringing it from the tin box in her pocket.

Hedgehog examined it, smelled at it and pinched it.

"If you use it, it will be gone, and there's an end of it. Take Old Hedgehog's advice and plant it. Then you'll maybe get a nutmeg tree," said he.

"That's just what I said," interrupted Hare. "I'm going to plant it now.

He dug a little hole and pushed the nutmeg down in the ground. Then he helped Squirrel to carry the washing-basket back to the house.

"My Missis will come and help with the ironing," said Hedgehog, as he put the milk on the doorstep. "She's a champion ironer and she seldom gets the chance to show her powers. Fuzzypeg will help Mister Hare to carry the clothes to their owners."

So Mrs Hedgehog came to iron the little garments. She brought with her a small flat-iron and a crimping-iron. Fuzzypeg sat watching his mother, and Grey Rabbit hung the things round the fire to air.

Then Hare went to Mole's house. He hung Mole's purple scarf on the holly tree near, and Moldy Warp had to get a ladder to reach it. He took Wise Owl's nightcap and tied it to the bell-rope of the beech tree where Wise Owl lived. He pinned the old mother rabbit's shawl to a gorsebush, and flung the youngest rabbit's nightgown into a robin's nest.

When the work was finished Hare and Fuzzypeg carried the piles of little garments back to the woods and commons. But of course Hare forgot where many of the things belonged. He dropped little handkerchiefs and mufflers and scarves and collars in every hole and door-way he could find. The mice and the dormice, the spider and the fly, the rabbits and squirrels, all got the wrong clothes. Even the butterfly got a tablecloth instead of his bedroom slippers.

All the little clothes were sprinkled about the fields, on bluebells and dandelions and primroses.

"Did you deliver the washing, Hare?" asked Grey Rabbit, when he came leaping in at the door.

"I got rid of it, Grey Rabbit," said Hare. "They will all find their clothes, if they look. They ought to be thankful for free washing, and nothing to pay."

"Oh Hare!" Grey Rabbit shook her head. "I did it for love."

"Hum!" said Hare. "Hum! Love!"

When Grey Rabbit lay in bed that night she heard a sound of singing in the lane. She ran to the window and leaned out. Along the path came the gipsy rabbit, but her fur was all silvery in the moonlight. She wore a shawl of rainbow gossamer, and in her ears hung the clusters of hazel catkins. On her head she bore the green rush basket, but whether it was filled with clothes-pegs or stars, Grey Rabbit couldn't be certain. They shone so brightly that the moon was dimmed by their light.

The gipsy glided past the garden wall, and her song came to Grey Rabbit's quick ears, although it was soft as a whisper.

"The gipsy walks the long road,
    Her basket on her head.
Her house is in the woodland,
    The bracken is her bed.

"Come buy my shining clothes-pegs,
    With bands of silver bound.
And peg your little apron,
    In orchard drying-ground.

"I bought the little clothes-pegs,
    With magic bells a-ringing.
I pegged my little apron,
    And the clothes began a-singing.

"I bought a little nutmeg,
    And set it in the ground.
A fine flowery nutmeg tree,
    Came springing from the mound."

"Too-whit, too-whoo!" hooted Wise Owl in the wood,
and the gipsy was silent. Nobody was to be seen, and
Grey Rabbit crept back to bed.

But the next day what do you think? There was a little nutmeg tree growing in the garden! It was covered with pink flowers and green leaves. When Hare ran out to look at it he found some brown nutmegs growing on the branches.

"A real gipsy, full of magic," said he, and Grey Rabbit and Squirrel agreed.

The End of the Story

Moldy Warp
the Mole

Moldy Warp sat in his armchair one morning, smoking his pipe of dried coltsfoot flowers, and examining a tiny square stone. He had found it in Hearthstone Pasture, when he had been walking in that high flowery field. It was painted with an eye, a golden eye, which seemed to watch the Mole wherever he went. It looked at him when he cooked his mushroom breakfast, when he made his hard little bed, and when he cleaned his spade and polished his pennies.

"Where this came from there will be the rest of the picture. There are only two creatures who could tell me about this eye," he continued musingly. "One is Wise Owl, who is asleep by day and fierce by night. I can't ask him. The other is Brock the Badger, and where he lives nobody knows. I haven't seen him for months, and he never takes a fellow to his house."

He washed the small stone in the stream which conveniently ran along the floor of his room, and he rubbed it on his sleeve.

"Now this is the picture of somebody's eye," said Mole to himself, "but it isn't a hare's or a squirrel's or a rabbit's. It's an ancient eye, an eye of long ago – before 1066. It belonged to somebody's picture-book, a stone picture-book." He polished it on his trousers and put it in his pocket.

While Moldy Warp was muttering to himself, he pottered about the room, putting the tobacco-box on the mantelpiece, tidying the table. Then he looked in his money-box. There lay the silver coin Hare had borrowed for "Turn the Trencher."

"I've not found any treasure since I made Owl's bell," thought Moldy Warp. "There isn't so much ploughing nowadays, and that man in corduroys is so clever with his traps I can't wander about just as I like. I'll go to Hearthstone Pasture and see if I can find anything more of the stone picture-book."

On the brown earthen walls hung some beautiful silver pennies, and on the shelf was a row of odds and ends Mole had found in the fields – a lead soldier with the paint off, a tin brooch, a pair of rusty scissors, and a threepenny bit. Mole loved the threepenny bit more than the fine coins. He had bored a hole through it, and he intended to give it to Grey Rabbit for her birthday.

He put a sod on the fire to keep it in. Then he took

his bright spade from the corner. There would be more digging to do than he could manage with his powerful hands and feet. He brushed his hair and whiskers and put on a clean collar. Then he washed his hands in the stream and looked at himself in a little bronze mirror which hung on the wall. Moldy Warp was a very particular little gentleman.

He went round his house to lock all the back doors. This took some time, for there were thirteen of them, each leading to a different molehill in Ten-acre Meadow.

He hung up his bunch of green sycamore keys on a peg and went down the passage to the front door. This led him out near the holly tree. He cut a short stick, peeled it to the smooth white inner, and started up the fields with the spade and a bag on his back.

He hadn't gone far when he saw an animal leaping across the field, careering this way and that, trying to catch his slender shadow.

"Hallo, Hare!" cried the Mole. "What's the matter?"

"I'm a mad March Hare!" shouted Hare. "I'm always like this when the March wind blows. I can't help it. It's my noble nature."

"But it's the month of May," objected Mole.

"It may be May! Ha! ha! There's a March wind, forgotten by somebody, blowing in this field. Do you know who my ancestor was, Moldy Warp?"

"Columbus Hare, the Explorer," answered Mole promptly.

"No, you're wrong. I'm descended from the famous Hare who raced the Tortoise in Old Æsop's day. I found him in a book Wise Owl lent to Grey Rabbit."

"Never heard of him," muttered Mole, and he walked away.

"If I had been there I should have won," continued Hare, leaping after and wagging his paw in Mole's face. "My ancestor lay down and slept, and the Tortoise won the race. Of course, Greece is a hot country."

"Never heard of it," mumbled Mole, plodding sturdily along.

Hare whisked round him. "Where are you going with that spade and sack, Moldy Warp?" he asked.

Mole hesitated. He didn't want Hare's company. Then his good temper overcame his discretion.

"I'm going treasure hunting," said he.

"Oh, Moldy Warp! Can I go with you?" Hare quivered with excitement.

"Yes," sighed Mole.

"I'll run ahead and save your short legs, Moldy," said Hare, and he galloped off and was soon out of sight, but Mole plodded slowly on his way.

In the next field a little figure stooped here and there, and Mole recognised little Grey Rabbit by her grey dress and white collar.

"Cuckoo!" he called. The rabbit looked up and then ran with a glad cry to meet him.

"I was gathering cowslips to make a cowslip ball,"

said she, and she showed her basket of flowers. "Where are you going, Moldy Warp?"

"I'm going on a treasure hunt," replied Mole.

"Can I come with you?" she asked. Then she stopped short. "It isn't like a Fox hunt, is it?"

"Not at all," said Mole. "It's rather like Hunt the Thimble, deep down in the ground."

Grey Rabbit walked by his side, talking of cowslip balls and cherry pie and fox's gloves. Every now and then she stopped to gather another cowslip, or she peered under the hedge at the Lords and Ladies in their green cloaks. Mole went solemnly on, and, with a light scutter of feet she caught him up.

Then Squirrel came bounding from a nut tree.

"Hallo! Where are you two going?"

"Treasure hunting," said Grey Rabbit happily. "Come along, Squirrel and help to carry it."

"I'm not dressed for treasure hunting," said Squirrel, and she stooped over a pool and stuck a cowslip in her dress. "I ought to have put on my new ribbon," she pouted.

She scampered eagerly after Grey Rabbit.

Shrill laughter and cries came from over the wall, and there, playing in the cornfield among the young green shoots was a company of small rabbits.

"Oats and Beans and Barley grows.
  Neither you nor anyone knows
  Where Oats and Beans and Barley grows,"

they sang, as they caught each other by the tail. They came scampering up to the Mole as he crawled through a hole in the wall.

"Please, Sir, what time is it?" they asked.

Before Mole could look at the sun Grey Rabbit replied,

"Half-past kissing-time,
  And time to kiss again."

All the little rabbits embraced each other, and rubbed their noses, and trotted after little Grey Rabbit, their friend.

"Where is Mole going?" they whispered.

"Sh-sh-sh," Grey Rabbit lowered her voice. "He's going treasure hunting," she said.

Mole led them through a shady lane along little private footpaths that only animals know.

"Wait for me! Don't leave me! Wait for me!" cried the youngest rabbit whose legs ached, and Grey Rabbit carried him pick-a-back for a time. The little procession passed through a field where cows were feeding.

Out of the thick grass came Hedgehog with his yoke across his shoulders and two pails of milk.

"Hallo! Moldy Warp, and little Grey Rabbit and Squirrel, and all you little 'uns! Where are you going so fast this morning?" he asked.

"Treasure hunting," replied Mole.

"I'll go along with you," said Hedgehog. "Come here, Fuzzypeg," he called. The shy little fellow came out of the grass with a butterfly net. "Come treasure-hunting. You can help to catch it if it flies away."

Fuzzypeg grinned and dropped behind. Soon they were joined by the Speckledy Hen, some field mice, a frog and a bumble-bee, all eager to hunt.

"There's rather a crowd," sighed Moldy Warp. "I shall be glad to get underground. For a retiring animal this is too much!"

At last they got to Hearthstone Pasture, where dark rocks lay on the smooth grass like black sheep.

"This is where I found my little square stone," Mole told them. "It was underneath the old hawthorn tree." He led them to a crooked thorn covered with snowy May blossom.

"Now wait while I go down and hunt for the treasure."

The animals sat round the tree in a circle and watched him. He took his sharp spade and began to dig. He seized his sack and wriggled down into the earth out of sight.

"Let us have a treasure hunt, too," cried Squirrel, "and Grey Rabbit shall give a prize."

So they all ran about the field peering among the rocks, poking their noses into crannies, sniffing and smelling and seeking.

One rabbit found a jay's feather, and another a wren's nest. Some found flowers and ladybirds, and one found a silk bag full of spider's eggs.

"Look what I've found," called Squirrel, and she

pointed to Hare, fast asleep under a rock.

"Where's the treasure?" he cried, rubbing his eyes.

"You are my treasure," laughed Squirrel.

"The prize is won by Fuzzypeg," announced little Grey Rabbit, and she took the little fellow by the paw and showed his find. It was a four-leaved clover, which, as everyone knows, is a lucky thing.

"What is the prize?" asked Hare anxiously.

"The Cowslip Ball," said Grey Rabbit, who had been industriously threading the cowslips on a grass. She gave the yellow flowery ball to Fuzzypeg, who tossed it up in the air and caught it.

"He's no butter-finger," said old Hedgehog.

"Butter? Butter? Where's Moldy Warp?" yawned Hare. "You promised macaroni cheese for supper, Grey Rabbit."

"The young rabbits ought to go home," said Grey Rabbit, "and Fuzzypeg and the Speckledy Hen. It's getting late."

"Oh no! Let us stay up to-night. We've never been up late," they implored. "Do let us stay, little Grey Rabbit."

"We can't desert old Mole," said Fuzzypeg.

"He will want us to carry his treasure," said a field-mouse.

"Perhaps he is lost," said the Speckledy Hen.

"Let us call him," suggested little Grey Rabbit. So they all put their paws to their mouths and gave the hide-and-seek cry, which all good children know.

"Cuckoo. Cherry-tree.

Moldy Warp, you can't see me."

"See me," replied a voice from the rocks, and the little rabbits looked scared.

"It's only the Echo," explained Hare, loftily. "It lives near here."

The Rooks flew cawing to the elms at Hearthstone Farm, the blackbirds sang their night song, and the blue veil of darkness slowly covered the fields.

The rabbits clustered round Grey Rabbit, and the youngest one clung to her skirt.

"I'm cold," he whimpered. "Can I come into your bed, Grey Rabbit?"

"I haven't got a bed," said little Grey Rabbit softly, and she put her arm round him. Then Wise Owl hooted, and far away a dog barked. Among the rocks there were little rustles, and Hedgehog bristled his spikes.

"Let us make a tent and all get inside," said Grey Rabbit.

Squirrel gathered long pointed leaves from a chestnut tree, and Hare stood on tiptoe to pull branches of flowery May. The field mice took their needles and cottons from their pockets, and sewed the leaves with tiny stitches, white and small as their own little teeth. Grey Rabbit pinned the strips together with thorn pins, and Hedgehog fixed a tent pole in the ground. Soon there was a fine leafy tent, sprinkled with hawthorn blossoms and prickly with thorns, standing in the field.

The Speckledy Hen laid an egg for Hedgehog's supper, and old Hedgehog gave everybody a drink of milk from his pails. The rabbits ate green bread-and-cheese, which grows on hawthorns, as every country child knows. Hare took some corn from his pocket and gave it to the Hen for her supper.

"I always carry corn in my purse," he boasted. "When I travel far I sprinkle it on the ground and thus find my way back."

"Don't the birds eat it?" asked the astonished rabbits, but Hare did not condescend to answer.

They all crept into the tent and cuddled together. Little Grey Rabbit told them the story of a White Rabbit named Cinderella, who went to a ball, and lost her glass slipper. In the end she married a Black Prince and lived happily ever after.

The little animals closed their eyes and fell asleep.

"Snuff! Sniff! Snuff-ff! I smell Rabbit," muttered a Red Fox.

"Sniff! Snuff! Sniff! I can't see Rabbit."

He glided round the little tent, smelling at it.

"Here's a little green bush where no tree used to be," he hissed. He put his long nose close to the leaves and opened his mouth.

"I'll puff and I'll huff and I'll blow their house down," he muttered. But the prickles of Old Hedgehog stuck in his chin, and the spikes of little Fuzzypeg scratched his

nose and the beak of the Speckledy Hen stabbed his eyes and all the thorns of the tent ran into his skin.

"It's a danger place, a trap for foxes, set by the keeper," grumbled the Red Fox, and he ran off to the farmyard, where bolts and bars foiled him again.

Now all this time Mole was underground. He went along smooth winding paths, up steps and down, through a little door and into a room. On the floor stood a stone crock filled with gold.

"Am I dreaming? Or is this Aladdin's cave?" he asked himself.

Footsteps padded near, and a large Badger entered the room.

"Moldy Warp! How did you get here! I've never had a visitor in all my life!" exclaimed the Badger, staring at Mole.

"Is this your house?" asked the astonished Mole. "I thought it was a treasure trove."

"It's my house and the house of my ancestors," said the Badger proudly. "For more than a thousand years we Badgers have lived here. Come and look round my castle, Mole."

He lighted a lantern and Mole blinked his dim eyes with amazement. The room was swept clean; stone benches and cupboards in the walls were all the furniture. On the floor was a picture of a blue and green dolphin, in an azure sea with glittering fish swimming around.

It was made of bright little square stones, but one tiny stone was missing. The lovely dolphin had only one eye.

Mole put his hand in his pocket and brought out his own little stone. It exactly fitted in the dolphin's head like a square in a puzzle.

"Mole, old fellow! Where did you find that? The missing eye, lost for many years!" cried Badger excitedly.

"Thank you! You are a clever chap, Mole! Only a wise Mole could have found the ancient Dolphin's eye."

He patted Mole so hard that the little animal fell over on the floor, and Badger had to pull him to his unsteady feet again.

Then Badger held up his lantern to a cupboard in the wall and showed Moldy Warp many a treasure of past ages. On the shelves were rows of tiny figures, of cocks and hens and hedgehogs and badgers, all carved out of coloured stones. There were flint arrow heads, gold necklaces and glass beads, polished and clean.

"How beautiful they are!" cried Mole.

"Many of them were left by the men who once lived in this house, and my ancestors found them there," said the Badger, holding the lantern aloft.

"Does anybody know about them?" asked Mole, wistfully. "Has anyone seen them?"

"No. They are safe down here, and I am their guardian," replied the hoary Badger. "You shall have a few to take to your own house, Moldy Warp."

Then Mole modestly chose a little grey stone rabbit, as big as a nut, and put it in his pocket, but the Badger lifted down little animals of jade and amber and dropped them into Mole's sack.

"They will do for doorstops for your fourteen doors, Moldy Warp," said he. "And here's the crock of gold, with a few coins for your walls. I have plenty of them."

Mole thanked him, and shook his great paw.

"Come and have some supper," said the Badger jovially.

He drew a jug of heather ale from a cask in the corner, and cut a hunk of sweet herb bread and some slices of cold ham.

He set two tankards on the stone table, and gave Mole a seat on the stone bench. Then, by the light of the horn lantern, the two ate and drank.

"Your health, Badger, Sir," said Mole, sipping the heather ale. "My! This is good!" He smacked his lips.

"Made from a long-forgotten recipe," said the Badger. "It is brewed from the heath and gorse flowers on the hills round here, picked when the honey is in the blossoms. Nobody but the Badger knows how to make it. Even Man has forgotten. I'll give you a pitcher of it to carry home."

Then the Badger talked of days long ago, when a brave race hunted with flint arrow heads. Later, the Romans came to England and made the stone picture

floors, such as Mole had seen, and always the Badger reigned in the woods. As he talked Mole's eyes began to close, his head nodded, and he dropped off to sleep.

When he awoke he lay in a truckle bed, tucked up with linen sheets. A glimmer of daylight came trickling through a cunning hole in the roof. He looked round for Badger, but the great animal had gone. Mole picked up his bag and crock, put the spade on his shoulder, and clasped the jug of heather ale.

He wandered along the confusing maze of passages, until at last he found himself in the open field, some distance away from where he had started.

He trotted as fast as he could to the hawthorn tree, calling, "Coo-oo. Coo-oo!"

"Somebody calling up the cows," yawned Hedgehog. He put his head through the tent opening and saw Mole.

"Here he is! Here's lost Moldy Warp!" he shouted, and the rest came tumbling after him into the field.

"Have you found the treasure, Moldy Warp?" they cried excitedly.

Mole opened his sack and emptied out the little cocks, the jade hedgehogs, the amber rabbits and a squirrel of green bronze.

"Oh my!" cried the little rabbits and fieldmice.

"Are they good to eat?" asked Hare, licking one.

"There's even hedgehogs among them," pondered Old Hedgehog happily.

"Where did you find these pretty toys?" asked Grey

Rabbit.

Mole shook his head. "Mum's the word," said he. "It's a secret that can never be told."

Then all the animals insisted on helping to carry his treasure. Each one took a precious little toy, and galloped off down the fields, leaving Moldy Warp to bring the crock of gold.

"Be careful!" he called. "Take care of them," but they ran faster than ever, eager to get home.

Some dropped their treasure in the long grass, and some lost them in the hedgerows. The field mice threw theirs away because they were too heavy. Hedgehog left his jade hedgehog in the cowshed, and the cow ate it with her hay.

Hare leaped over a gorse bush and the amber hare fell from his pocket. Squirrel put her bronze squirrel on a wall and forgot about it. The Speckledy Hen dropped her gold hen in the corn.

Little Grey Rabbit carried the pitcher of heather ale without spilling a drop. She left it at Mole's front door by the holly tree, and hurried home to cook breakfast for Squirrel and Hare.

"Ah me!" sighed the Mole, when he arrived hours later. "I'm glad I carried my crock of gold myself. Careless scatter-brained folk!" He waddled slowly into his pantry with the heather ale.

"That's safe, thanks to Grey Rabbit," said he, as he tasted the honey brew.

He washed a few of his coins in the stream and dried them on his handkerchief. Then he polished them on his fur sleeve till they shone like lamps.

He hung them on the walls and looked admiringly at the pictures of eagles and lions and men which were engraved upon them.

There was a rat-tat-tat at the door and he went to open it.

"They are all very sorry they lost your treasures, Moldy Warp," said little Grey Rabbit, stepping in with Old Hedgehog's milk pail full of flowers. "They have sent you these instead."

She filled a jug with silver daisies, and golden butter-cups, and little amber-coloured pansies, and jade green orchis.

"They are quite as nice, aren't they, Moldy Warp? You like them just as much, don't you?" she asked wistfully.

"More, much more," answered the Mole. "What is a precious stone to a living flower?" Yet he gave a deep sigh.

He put his hand in his pocket and brought out his forgotten little stone rabbit. He put it in the middle of the mantelpiece and Grey Rabbit stood on tiptoes to look at it.

"It's just like me," said she.

"I'm going to give a picnic to all the animals who kindly waited for me in that cold wild pasture up there

on the hill," said Mole. "Please ask them to come to-morrow afternoon to the holly tree by my front door, Grey Rabbit."

Little Grey Rabbit bobbed a curtsey of thanks and ran to spread the good news.

The next day they all appeared, dressed in their best clothes. There was Mole ready for them, with the table-cloth spread out on the daisies and the jug of flowers in the middle. Little Grey Rabbit carried a basketful of cowslip balls to play with after tea, and Fuzzypeg had a cricket bat, which his father had made.

Mole had provided wild raspberries and honeycomb, rose-petal jam, bluebell jelly, lettuces and tiny red carrots. There was even a dish of golden corn for the Speckledy Hen, who came in her best Paisley shawl and her little black bonnet.

"Very forgiving, I call it, when we lost his treasure," said she to Old Hedgehog, who had brought Mrs Hedgehog with him.

"He's a kind-hearted gentleman," answered Hedge-hog, and he put a can of cream on the cloth.

"My compliments, Sir," said he.

"Your very good health, Moldy Warp," called Hare, as he sipped the heather ale which filled the tiny glasses.

"Good health! Good luck!" cried the others, all drinking the ancient sun-filled honey ale.

Mole nodded and smiled and sat back with his velvet coat glossy in the sunshine.

What a lot of good friends he had, to be sure!

The End of the Story

Fuzzypeg
Goes to School

It was bedtime and little Fuzzypeg the Hedgehog sat by the fire in his nightgown eating his bread and milk. His mother was mending his blue smock which he had torn on his prickles.

"Will my father tell me a tale to-night?" asked Fuzzypeg.

"If you're a good hedgehog and eat every bit of your supper," said Mrs Hedgehog kindly.

Old Hedgehog hung up his milking-yoke and came into the cosy room.

"Please tell me a bedtime story," implored Fuzzypeg. Old Hedgehog rubbed his hands and scratched his head, trying to think of a nice tale. Then he began to chant the song of the Frog.

"A Frog he would a-wooing go,
Whether his mother would let him or no,
Heigho! says Rowley."

Fuzzypeg beat time with his spoon on the wooden bowl, and Mrs Hedgehog forgot to thread her needle as she listened. When he had sung the poem, Mrs Hedgehog took a length of thread, and Fuzzypeg finished his supper.

"What a lovely tale!" cried Fuzzypeg.

"How clever you are, my dear!" Mrs Hedgehog exclaimed.

"I learned that in my schooldays, when I was a youngster, same as Fuzzypeg," said Hedgehog modestly.

"Can I go to school and learn poems?" asked Fuzzypeg.

"I think he is big enough, don't you, Hedgehog?" And Mrs Hedgehog looked at her husband.

"Yes, it's about time he had some eddication," replied Hedgehog.

"You can't get on without some kind of wisdom. Just think what a lot Wise Owl knows!"

"And Miss Squirrel and Little Grey Rabbit," said Mrs Hedgehog.

"And Hare," added Fuzzypeg. "He taught me to play noughts and crosses that day I got lost."

"That's not wisdom," explained Hedgehog. "That's rubbidge."

"Can I go to school to-morrow? Please! Please!" Fuzzypeg asked, jumping down from his stool.

"Yes, if I've mended these holes in time," Mrs Hedge-hog told him, and Fuzzypeg hopped round the room for joy. Then he went to the door to say good-night to the world.

"Good-night, star," he called to the evening star, and it nodded good-night and hid behind a cloud, for it was shocked that Fuzzypeg wasn't asleep.

Fuzzypeg shut the door, kissed his parents and went upstairs.

The next morning he awoke early and sprang out of bed in a great hurry.

"I'm going to school to-day," he sang, as he rolled downstairs in a prickly ball and bounced into the room where Mrs Hedgehog was cooking the breakfast.

Old Hedgehog had been out since dawn, milking the cows and carrying milk to his customers.

Fuzzypeg saw him returning across the croft, so he ran to meet him. The hedgehog carried something under his arm, and Fuzzypeg danced round, asking what it was.

"Wait a minute. Don't be in such a harum-scarum-hurry! It might bite you!" said Old Hedgehog, smiling.

He gave Mrs Hedgehog the milk for breakfast and then he sat down and slowly opened the parcel.

He took from the leafy paper a little leather bag, and Fuzzypeg turned it over with shrill cries of excitement.

"A school-bag! A school-bag! Look, Mother! Where

117

has it come from?"

He showed Mrs Hedgehog all the pockets. There was a big pocket for sandwiches, and two little ones for lesson books, and a tiny one for the penny to pay for the schooling.

"Grey Rabbit gave it to me when she heard you were going to school," said Hedgehog. "I took the milk as usual this morning, and Miss Grey Rabbit, she sez to me, sez she, 'You're looking very perky this morning, Hedgehog. Has something happened?' So I tells her, 'My little Fuzzypeg's going to school,' sez I. 'He's going to get wisdom, same as Wise Owl,' sez I. 'Indeed!' sez she. 'This is a great day for you, Hedgehog, and a greater one for little Fuzzypeg.'

" 'Wait a minute,' sez she. So I stood on the doorstep, and then Grey Rabbit comes downstairs, and she was carrying this.

" 'A lesson bag for Fuzzypeg,' sez she.

" 'And I hope he'll bag his lessons in it,' sez Hare.

" 'And the more he bags, the less there'll be,' sez Squirrel; but I was moithered by the clever talk and I hurried home."

"What shall I put in it?" asked Fuzzypeg, turning it inside out.

"Your lessons – sums and poems and tales," said Hedgehog, "and your sandwiches for elevens, and your penny for the schoolmaster."

Then they all had a good breakfast, and Fuzzypeg

started off for school with the leather bag on his back.

As he went down the lane he saw his cousins, Tim and Bill Hedgehog, who lived in the cottage in the larch wood.

"Hallo, Fuzzypeg!" they called.

"Where are you going with that fine bag?"

"I'm going to school," said Fuzzypeg proudly.

"Wait a minute. We'll come too," cried the little hedgehogs, and they ran quickly to their mother who was shaking the table-cloth to the ants in the larch wood.

"Mother! Mother!" they shouted excitedly. "Can we go to school with Fuzzypeg?"

"Yes. If Fuzzypeg is big enough, so are you," said their mother.

"It mustn't be said that my children are not as clever as Fuzzypeg!"

She brushed their quills and tidied their smocks, and cut their sandwiches, and sent them off.

"I say, do be quick, you fellows," called Fuzzypeg through the doorway. "We shall be late."

"Late? What's late?" asked Tim.

"I don't know. Something we mustn't be," replied Fuzzypeg.

"I 'specks we shall learn all about it at school."

They trotted along the lane, when who should they see but Hare, lolloping along in his bright blue coat.

"Hallo, Fuzzypeg! Hallo, young 'uns!" he called. "Have you seen it? I've lost it again."

"No," said the little hedgehogs, shaking their heads.

"Seen what?" asked Fuzzypeg.

"Yes, seen what?" echoed Tim and Bill.

"My shadow. It's not anywhere about. I don't know where I put it."

"Perhaps it is in Robin Postman's nest," suggested Fuzzypeg, and he knocked at the door of a neat nest in the daisied bank.

"Yes, what is the matter?" asked the postman.

"Have you seen Hare's shadow anywhere about?" asked Fuzzypeg.

"No. Has he lost it?" The little postman stared at Hare and then he looked up at the sky.

"Of course he hasn't a shadow," Robin exclaimed. "None of you have shadows."

The three hedgehogs looked behind and before them.

"No, we haven't. Oh, dear! We can't go to school without shadows!" they cried.

"Wait till the sun comes out, and then your shadows will leap back to you," advised the Robin, and he went in and shut his door, for he had some leafy letters to sort.

"What is inside your bag, Fuzzypeg?" Hare asked.

"Sandwiches," replied Fuzzypeg, and he brought them out and divided them.

"Now you've plenty of room for other things," said Hare, and they gathered bindweed, forget-me-nots, eye-bright, foxgloves.

"Those are all lessons," said Hare, "and if you'll sit

121

down on this bank I will teach you your ABC."

All the animals came close to him and listened very hard.

"A. Hay grows in the Daisy Field, when the sun shines and the mowers come," said Hare.

"I like Hay. I helped to make it once with Grey Rabbit," said little Fuzzypeg.

"B. Bees live in gardens and come buzzing and humming at you. They get honey and that is a very good thing," said Hare.

"I've been stung by a Bee," said Tim Hedgehog.

"C. Seas are very wet, very wet indeed. They are all water and they never dry up," said Hare.

"I shouldn't like to fall in C," said Fuzzypeg, and the others agreed. "No, we don't like C," said they.

"That's all for to-day. You know your ABC," said Hare, suddenly springing to his feet and running off, for he had spied Little Grey Rabbit coming towards them.

Little Grey Rabbit came tripping along the path, with her basket on her arm. When she saw the three little hedgehogs sitting on the grass, she was astonished.

"What are you doing here, Fuzzypeg?" she asked. "I thought you were at school."

"Please, Grey Rabbit, we are waiting for the sun to come out. We can't go to school without our shadows."

"Of course you can! Now run along, as fast as you can, or your teacher will be very cross."

So off they ran, under the gate, to Daisy Field, and across that lovely flower-filled meadow to the little pasture where Jonathan Rabbit had his school. A sweet tinkle, tinkle, came from the field.

"That's the school bell," said the Thrush. "You'll be late. Young Hare always rings the hare-bells, you know. He's been jingling them a long time now."

So they ran, puffing and panting, towards the sound of the blue bells, which floated like delicate music from a house hidden in the gorse bushes.

They pushed aside a leafy curtain, walked along a passage through the gorse and knocked at a little green door with a brass knocker, hidden in the low bushes. The door swung open, and they entered a room, whose walls were made of closely-woven blackberry bushes and wild roses, whose floor was the soft fragrant turf of the pasture, starred with wild thyme, and blue milk-wort, and sweet clover, growing over it like a pattern in a carpet.

The ceiling of the schoolroom was the blue sky, where the sun was now shining, so that the little hedgehogs saw their shadows at their side as they walked shyly across the room to Old Jonathan.

"Benjamin Hedgehog.

"Timothy Hedgehog.

"Fuzzypeg Hedgehog," said he.

He wrote their names on a rose-leaf, in squiggly letters. "Each of you is

'A diller, a dollar,
 A ten-o'clock scholar.'
"Remember that school begins at nine o'clock, and don't be late!"

They sat down on the mossy bank which ran round the room, by the side of several little animals – hedgehogs, squirrels, rabbits, the young hare, a small mole and some field mice. They all read from books made of green leaves, which Jonathan gave them.

Then he asked them some questions, and all the little animals stood up in a row, with Fuzzypeg at the end.

"Which flower helps a rabbit to remember?" he asked.

Nobody knew the answer, but little Fuzzypeg drew the blue forget-me-nots from his lesson bag and held them up.

"Quite right, Fuzzypeg. Go to the top of the class," said Jonathan approvingly.

"Which flower shuts its eyes when it rains?" he asked. All the little animals shut their eyes and tried forget-me-notting, but Fuzzypeg held up the white trumpet of the climbing bindweed.

Then Jonathan asked his last question. "Which flower makes gloves for cold paws?"

Every animal knew the answer, and they all shouted at the tops of their voices, "Foxgloves," before Fuzzypeg could get the purple foxglove from the bottom of the satchel.

125

"Now for a counting lesson," Jonathan continued.

"One, two, buckle my shoe," sang the animals, and all the little hedgehogs fastened their shoe latchets, but the squirrels and the mole and the rest who wore no shoes had to look on.

"Three, four, knock at the door," they sang.

They ran to knock on the brass knocker, tat-tatting like a postman.

"Five, six, pick up sticks," they sang, and they all ran into the pasture and gathered as many sticks and twigs as they could carry.

"Seven, eight, lay them straight," they sang, and each tried to lay his sticks in even lengths, which was very difficult.

Now Jonathan had enough sticks for his fire, so they put them in a pile and lighted them.

Then, whilst he rested from his labours, he sent the little animals out to play.

"Eleven o'clock," said he, blowing at a dandelion clock. "Go and eat your sandwiches."

Suddenly Fuzzypeg saw a little figure in a grey dress with white collar and cuffs coming across Daisy Field towards the school.

"Here's Little Grey Rabbit!" called all the animals, and they rushed to meet her and begged her to sit down and tell them a story.

She sat on a tuffet in the shade of a hawthorn-tree and began the tale of Red Riding Hood. She had just got to

the part where Red Riding Hood came to her grand-mother's cottage and pulled down the bobbin, and all the little animals were pressed close to her, their eyes wide open, their ears listening to every word she spoke, when there was a mighty roaring noise close by, from behind the hawthorn-tree.

"Woof! Woof! Woof! I'll nab you," it said, in a terrible deep voice.

"Oh! Oh! Oh!" shrieked the little hedgehogs and squirrels and field mice, and hare and mole. "Oh! The Wolf!"

"Boo! Boo! Woof!" came the strange voice so close they felt the creature was upon them.

"It's the Wolf!" they shouted, and they all ran helter-skelter, up and down the field, seeking for shelter.

Grey Rabbit stood very still, for she thought she recognised the voice, though it was different in some way.

"Woof! Woof! I'll nab you," roared the creature gruffly.

"Come out, Hare," said Grey Rabbit sternly. "Hare! Naughty Hare! Come out at once! I know that voice! You can't deceive me."

From behind the tree leaped Hare, holding a cone-shaped trumpet, made from the bark of the silver birch-tree.

"Ha! Ha! I frightened you. You thought it was a wolf, didn't you?"

"I guess old Jonathan didn't know all the uses of the silver birch-tree when he taught you your lessons."

All the little animals came creeping out, to stare at the trumpet which Hare carried; all except the youngest rabbit, who was far away, galloping along the leafy lanes home, and Fuzzypeg.

"Where's Fuzzypeg?" asked Little Grey Rabbit.

"Where's Fuzzypeg?" echoed the others.

Then they heard a squeaky little voice. "A-tishoo!" it said. "Help! A-tishoo! A-shoo!"

From out of the stream crawled a very bedraggled little hedgehog, with his satchel on his back and his smock all covered with water weeds.

"C is very wet," he said.

"A-tishoo!"

"Poor little Fuzzypeg," said Grey Rabbit, running up to him. "You'd better go straight home to bed."

"School, dismiss!" shouted Jonathan. "A holiday. No more school to-day. You've done quite enough lessons."

And the little animals all leaped up and down, crying: "A holiday!"

"I didn't want a holiday. I've only just begun," said Fuzzypeg in a quavering voice. "A-tishoo!"

But Grey Rabbit took him by the hand and hurried him home, whilst Hare ran alongside.

"Whatever have you been and gone and done?" asked Mrs Hedgehog, holding up her hands in horror when she saw her wet little son.

Little Grey Rabbit explained what had happened, and Hare said, "I'm very sorry, Mrs Hedgehog. It shan't occur again. My high spirits got the better of me. I had found my shadow, and it went to my head." Then he ran away, leaping home.

"You must put Fuzzypeg to bed at once, Mrs Hedgehog," said Grey Rabbit.

So little Fuzzypeg was popped into his warm bed, with a bowl of delicious gruel and black-currant tea.

Grey Rabbit sat at his bedside, and she sang little songs to him, while Fuzzypeg sneezed and chuckled, and sneezed again.

Then Hare put his head in at the door. "I've brought you some of my treacle toffee," said he. "I made it myself, so you may be sure it is nice. It's a fine cure for a sore throat. I'm sorry you fell in the water, Fuzzypeg, old chap."

"He will soon be better," said Grey Rabbit. "I'll come home with you now, Hare. Good-bye, Fuzzypeg."

Fuzzypeg croaked, "Good-bye, Grey Rabbit. Good-bye, Hare." And then he shut his eyes and slept till his father came home.

"What did they larn you besides swimming, my son?" asked Old Hedgehog, as he stood at the bedside looking at little Fuzzypeg, muffled up in his blankets.

"Straw, Wasps and Ponds," said Fuzzypeg dreamily.

"No, Father, I don't think that was what Hare taught

me. It was Hay, Bee and Sea. I fell into C, Father. And to-morrow we are going to learn 'Here we go gathering nuts in May,' and I'm going to have the youngest rabbit for my nuts in May. I like school, Father."

"You've not larned much," said Old Hedgehog, "and they say, 'A little larning is a dangerous thing.'

"You'd better get a bit more knowledge to-morrow, and don't go to Mr Hare for your lessons, neither."

The End of the Story

Little Grey Rabbit's Christmas

It had been snowing for hours.

Hare stood in the garden of the little house at the end of the wood, watching the snowflakes which came softly tumbling down like white feathers. His paws were outstretched, his head uplifted, his mouth wide open. His fur was sprinkled with snow, so that he looked like a white Hare from the icy North. Every now and then he caught an extra large flake and ate it with relish.

"Whatever are you doing, Hare?" cried Squirrel, who sat close to the fire. "Come in! You'll catch cold."

"I am catching cold, and eating it, too," replied Hare happily.

"Hare! How long do you think she will be? Can you see her coming?" called Squirrel again.

Hare slowly turned his head to the door.

"Did you speak, Squirrel, or did you merely squeak?"

135

he asked.

"I speaked," said Squirrel, indignantly. "I mean to say I spoke! Where is little Grey Rabbit?"

"She's at the market, buying Christmas fare for all of us," replied Hare. "I think she is choosing something special for me. I want barley sugar, peppermint rock, a musical box——"

As he spoke a small stout animal came trudging up the lane, laden with a heavy basket, and a string bag bulging with knobs. Straggling behind was a little snow-covered creature.

"There she is!" cried Hare, leaping forward. "Make the tea, Squirrel."

He ran down the path, and then stopped, disappointed.

"It's only Mrs Hedgehog!" he muttered.

"And Fuzzypeg," he added as he recognised the little fellow.

"Yes, it's only me," grunted Mrs Hedgehog wearily, and she shook the snow from her cape.

"And me," piped Fuzzypeg.

"Have you seen little Grey Rabbit?" asked Hare, as he leaned over the gate.

Mrs Hedgehog rested her burden on the snow and wiped her face.

"I have indeed. She was at the market along of me. Then she went to talk to Old Joe the Carpenter."

"What did she want with Joe?" asked Hare.

"She went inside his shed, and I hurried away, for I had to get my Christmas fairings. I didn't wait for Grey Rabbit."

"Please Sir!" cried little Fuzzypeg. "I knows, Sir. I knows what Grey Rabbit went to the carpenter for, Mister Hare. It was for——"

"Sh-sh!" Mrs Hedgehog shook her head at her son. "You mustn't let the cat out of the bag. Miss Grey Rabbit wouldn't like it."

Hare looked alarmed, but Mrs Hedgehog picked up her basket.

"I must be getting along, or my old man won't get his apple-dumplings for tea," said she, and away she went, with little Fuzzypeg protesting:

"There wasn't a cat in the bag, Mother. There wasn't."

It was growing dark when Squirrel and Hare heard the sound of merry voices and the ringing of bells in the lane. They ran to the door, and what should they see but a fine scarlet sledge drawn by two young rabbits, and little Grey Rabbit herself sitting cosily on the top!

The sledge stopped at the door and Grey Rabbit sprang off and curtsied to her astonished friends.

"That's a fine contraption!" exclaimed Hare, admiringly. "Where did you hire it?"

"Oh, Grey Rabbit! What a lovely cart!" cried Squirrel. She rubbed her paws over the smooth sides and peered at the holly leaves which adorned the sledge.

"Grey Rabbit! Our names are on it!" shouted Hare.

He pointed excitedly to the words, "Squirrel, Hare, and Little Grey Rabbit," written in flowing rabbity letters round the sides.

"It's ours! It says so!"

"Yes, it is our very own," answered Grey Rabbit. "I ordered it from Joe Carpenter, but I had to wait for the paint to dry. These kind rabbits insisted on bringing me home on it. We will go out sledging tomorrow."

The two rabbits stamped their feet to rid them of the snow, and little Grey Rabbit gathered up her parcels.

"Come inside and have a glass of primrose wine," she invited them, and they stepped shyly after her.

Squirrel fetched the yellow wine, and Grey Rabbit took a couple of acorn glasses from the cupboard.

Hare remained at the door murmuring to himself. "It's just what I wanted. The very thing for me! If anyone had said to me, 'Hare, old chap! What would you like best in all the world?' I should answer, 'A scarlet-coloured sledge.'"

"With bells on it," added Squirrel, who overheard him.

"And our names on the sides," continued Hare, dreamily.

"A Merry Christmas when it comes," said the two rabbits, raising their glasses to little Grey Rabbit.

"The same to you and many of them," replied Grey Rabbit.

They drank the flower-tasting wine, and then ran off

down the lane to their home, to tell their mother all about the fine sledge.

Grey Rabbit untied her parcels and put away her groceries. Some little packets she hid, but Squirrel and Hare were too busy wiping the snow from the new sledge and examining the runners to pay any heed to Grey Rabbit and her secrets.

After breakfast the next day they set off. Squirrel and little Grey Rabbit sat on the sledge, and Hare pulled them over the field.

They came to their favourite hill. Hare mounted behind them, and stretched out his long legs to guide them.

"One to be ready!

"Two to be steady!

"Three to be OFF!" he cried, and away they went down the steep slope, shouting with excitement, clinging to one another as the sledge gathered speed. It flew like a streak of lightning.

"Whoo-oo-oo!" cried Hare breathlessly. "What a speed! What an express train! Whoops! Whoa! Whoa, mare!"

But the sledge wouldn't stop!

At last it struck a mole-hill, and over they all toppled, little furry bodies tumbling head over heels.

"Where am I?" asked Squirrel faintly.

"In a goose-feather bed," laughed Grey Rabbit, shaking herself.

"Sixty miles an hour!" cried Hare, sitting up and rubbing his elbow.

Little Fuzzypeg, carrying a slice of bread and jam for his lunch, came to watch the fun.

He stared at the three dragging their pretty sledge up the slope, and he longed to join them.

"I want to toboggan," said he softly, but nobody heard. Squirrel, Hare and little Grey Rabbit settled themselves on the seat and started on another journey.

"Look at *me* toboggan! Watch *me*!" cried Fuzzypeg. He made himself into a ball and rolled down the hill, faster and faster. When he got to the bottom there was no Fuzzypeg to be seen, only an enormous snowball.

"What a big snowball!" cried Squirrel, climbing off the sledge and shaking her dress as the snowball bumped alongside.

"What a beauty!" exclaimed Grey Rabbit, admiringly.

"Help! Help!" squeaked a tiny muffled voice. "Get me out!"

"What's that?" cried Squirrel, startled. "I thought I heard a sound."

"Help! Help!" piped little Fuzzypeg faintly.

"That's a talking snowball," explained Hare, leaning over the great ball. "Isn't it interesting? Has anyone ever seen a snowball that could talk? I don't expect Wise Owl for all his cleverness has seen such a thing! Isn't it a curiosity! I'll take it home and keep it in the garden."

He dragged the large ball on to the sledge, and pulled the load uphill. Squirrel and Grey Rabbit wondered where the snowball had come from, and whether the Snow Queen had dropped it from the clouds.

When they reached the top Hare rolled the ball to the ground and gave it a kick.

"Ugh!" he cried, limping. "There's a thorn inside."

"Help! Help!" shrieked the tiny faraway voice indignantly. "Lemme out!"

"That is like Fuzzypeg's voice," said Grey Rabbit, with a puzzled frown, and she bent over and loosened the caked snow.

Out came the little hedgehog, eating his bread and jam.

"However did you get inside a snowball?" asked Hare, who was most disappointed at this discovery.

"I didn't get inside. It got round me," replied Fuzzypeg calmly. "Can I go on your sledge now?"

"Hare will take you," promised little Grey Rabbit. "There won't be room for us all with your needles and pins."

Hare took the little hedgehog for a ride, but when Fuzzypeg flung his arms round Hare's waist, he sprang shrieking away.

"That's enough!" said he severely. "My motto is 'Never go hedging with a sledgehog.'"

"I mean to say," he corrected himself hastily,

" 'Never go sledging with a hedgehog.' You must ride alone, young fellow."

Fuzzypeg ran home and returned with a tea-tray. After him came a crowd of rabbits, each carrying a tray and they all rode helter-skelter down the slope, shouting and laughing as they tried to race each other.

Squirrel, Hare and little Grey Rabbit took their sledge to Moldy Warp's house. The holly trees were ablaze with red berries, and Squirrel ran up the trees and gathered some sprays. Mole came out to show them the lovely pale branches of mistletoe growing on an oak tree.

He pointed out some of the beauties of the snowy wood, the crystal ice-caverns where icicles hung like spears, the snow garden with glittering white flowers, the ice bridges which spanned the ditches, the snow castles with towers, all made by Jack Frost, the clever Smith from the North Pole.

Then he said good-bye, for it was Christmas Eve, and everyone had work to do, in preparation for the Day.

Hare shut the sledge in the wood-shed and carried the holly and mistletoe indoors. He began to decorate the room, helped by the nimble Squirrel. Little Grey Rabbit stood at the table, her cooking apron wrapped round her, making mince-pies.

"Is that right, Grey Rabbit? Shall we hang some holly here?" asked Hare, as Squirrel popped sprigs over

144

the corner cupboard, and round the warming-pan, and among the mugs on the dresser.

Little Grey Rabbit looked up from the tin patty-pans, and waved her rolling-pin, to direct the operations.

The fire crackled in the chimney, sweet smells filled the kitchen – the scent of the burning logs, and the smell of dried lavender which hung from the ceiling, and the fragrance of the green holly which Hare carried.

The silver moon shone down on the white fields, making them glitter with a strange and beautiful light. The stars twinkled in the frosty air, and now and then a shooting star left a track of gold across the heavens.

Up the lane came a little company, carrying rolls of music and pipes of straw. Their tiny feet made crackles in the snow, and they talked softly as they walked up to the closed door of Grey Rabbit's house.

"You strike up first, Brush," said one of the rabbits. "Your voice is the powerfullest."

"No, it ain't," said Brush, a hoary old hedgehog, whose bristles were thick as a broomhead. "I'm hoarse as a crow. You start, Milkman Hedgehog."

"Not me," cried Hedgehog, shaking his head. "I've lost my top notes, and bottom ones too. I can't start."

"Let me," interrupted Fuzzypeg, but his father nudged him.

"You wait till you're axed and let your elders and betters sing first," said he sternly.

"Now then, altogether!" cried an important-looking

145

rabbit, playing a note on his straw pipe. "One, two, three!" and with their noses in the air, the company began to sing in small squeaky voices this Christmas carol:

"Holly red and mistletoe white,
    Peace on earth and mercy bright,
A truce by the tree of candle-light,
    Holly red and mistletoe white.

Mistletoe white and holly red,
    The day is over, we're off to bed,
Tired body and sleepy head,
    Mistletoe white and holly red."

"Hush! What's that noise?" cried Hare, dropping his mistletoe and listening.

"It's the Waits!" said little Grey Rabbit, and she held up her wooden spoon.

They flung wide the door and saw the little group of rabbits and hedgehogs peering at their sheets of music.

"Come in! Come in!" cried Grey Rabbit. "Come and sing by the fireside. You look frozen with the cold."

"We're all right," answered Brush, "but a warm drink would wet our whistles. Some of us have lost our voices on the way here."

"So I thought," whispered Hare to Squirrel.

Grey Rabbit took from the fire the two-handled Christmas mug of mulled primrose wine, and the

carollers passed it round.

"That's better," sighed Old Hedgehog. "Thank 'ee kindly. Now we shan't be so hoarse. I tell 'ee, my voice was like a key turning in a rusty lock!"

They stood by the fire and sang all the songs they knew, such as "The Moon shines bright," and "I saw three ships a-sailing," and "Green grows the holly."

"Now we must be off," said they, when little Grey Rabbit had given them hot mince-pies. "We have to sing at all the rabbit houses on the common. Good night! The compliments of the season! Happy Christmas and many of them."

"The same to you," replied Hare politely, and he opened the door. Squirrel and Grey Rabbit stood by him, watching the Waits as they took the field path, listening to the carol, "Holly red and Mistletoe white," which the animals sang as they trotted along.

"I think I shall take out the sledge and toboggan down the hill by moonlight," said Hare, looking up at the round moon which made the land bright as day. "I might see something of Santa Claus and his reindeer."

He wrapped a muffler round his neck, seized the cord of the sledge and ran across the fields to the hill.

Then down he swooped, flying like a bird.

Everything looked different in the white moonbeams. The ice crackled, the stars sparkled blue and green and winked at the excited Hare. Again and again he rushed down the hill, his eyes on the lovely moon. Suddenly he noticed a dark shadow running alongside. It was his own moon-shadow, but Hare saw the long ears and the round head of a strange monster.

"Oh dear! Oh dear! Who is that dusky fellow racing by my side?" he cried.

He took to his heels, leaving the sledge lying in the field, and away he went, as fast as he could, running from his own long shadow.

"Did you come home without the sledge?" asked Squirrel indignantly. "Hare! You are a coward! I don't believe there was anybody at all. You ran away from your shadow! You've lost our lovely sledge!"

"Better than losing my lovely life," retorted Hare. He felt rather miserable. He wished he had stopped to look at the dusky creature which chased him. Shadows were good companions, and he had run away, and deserted the scarlet sledge.

"I suppose we had better go to bed," he muttered. "I don't suppose there will be any presents tomorrow. I don't think Santa Claus will find this house with so much snow about!"

He went upstairs gloomily, but he hung up his furry stocking all the same, and so did Squirrel.

When all was quiet, Grey Rabbit crept out of her room and peeped at Hare lying fast asleep. Then she looked at Squirrel, whose tail was curled over her eyes. She ran back to her own room. Under the bed was a store of parcels. She opened them and filled the stockings with sugar-plums and lollipops, and placed little gifts at the foot of each bed. Then she ran downstairs to the kitchen, where the dying fire flickered softly.

She tied together little sprays of holly and made a round ball called a Kissing Bunch. She decked it with scarlet crab-apples and gilded nuts, all dangling among the glossy green leaves. Then she hung it from a hook in the ceiling.

"Won't they be surprised!" she chuckled to herself.

On Christmas morning Grey Rabbit was so sleepy she didn't wake till Hare burst into her room.

"Grey Rabbit! Merry Christmas! Grey Rabbit!"

"Merry Christmas, Hare," murmured the little rabbit.

"Grey Rabbit! He's been! Wake up! He's been in the night!"

"Who?" cried Grey Rabbit, rubbing her eyes and sitting up in a fright. "Who? Has Rat been?"

"Santa Claus!" cried Hare, capering up and down by her bed. "Be quick and come downstairs and see the surprises."

Grey Rabbit dressed hurriedly, but there was a little twinkle in her eyes as she entered the room.

"Look what he brought me!" cried Squirrel, holding out a pair of fur mittens and bedroom slippers made from sheep's wool.

"And he gave me a spotted handkerchief, and a

musical box," cried Hare excitedly, and he turned the handle of the little round box from which came a jolly tune which set their feet dancing.

"Look at the Kissing Bunch!" Hare went on. "Isn't it lovely! Let's all kiss under it."

So they gave their Christmas morning kisses under the round Christmas Bunch in the time-honoured way.

Robin the Postman flew to the door with some Christmas cards and a letter. The little bird rested and ate some breakfast while Hare examined the leaf with its tiny pointed scribble.

"It's from Mole," said he, twisting it over and over.

"Yes, I know," replied Robin. "Mole gave it to me."

"You're reading it upside down, Hare," cried Squirrel impatiently. She took the little letter and read the scrawl.

"Come to-night. Love from Moldy Warp."

"It's a party!" cried Hare. "Quick, Grey Rabbit! Write and say we'll all be there, and we hope there will be plenty to eat."

Grey Rabbit sat at her desk and wrote in careful letters on an ivy leaf, "Thank you, Dear Moldy Warp."

Then away flew the Robin, with the leaf in his bag.

"Let us take some mince-pies to Moldy Warp," said Grey Rabbit.

"And my last year's spotted handkerchief," said Hare.

All day they enjoyed themselves, playing "Musical Chairs" to the tunes in Hare's musical box, pulling the tiny crackers from the gorse-bush, crunching the lolli-pops. Grey Rabbit read aloud the story of Cinderella; Squirrel sang a carol; and Hare did some conjuring tricks.

They all trooped to the hill to look for the sledge, but it wasn't there. Snow had covered all traces of footprints.

"Santa Claus has borrowed it," Grey Rabbit con-soled Hare. "When the snow melts we shall find it."

The first star appeared in the sky, and the three animals wrapped themselves up in warm clothes, and started for Mole's house.

"What a pity you lost our beautiful sledge! We could have ridden on it to-night," said Squirrel to Hare.

Hare hung his head. He wished she wouldn't talk about it so much.

When the three got near Mole's house they saw some-thing glittering. A lighted tree grew by the path, like a burning beacon.

"Oh dear! Something's on fire!" cried Hare. "Let's put it out. Climb up and blow it out, Squirrel!"

"Hush!" whispered Grey Rabbit. "It's a magical tree, a tree from Fairyland growing in our wood!"

On every branch of the little fir-tree candles wavered their tongues of flame. Little red and gold fruits hung from the tips of the boughs. On the ground under the branches were bowls of hazel nuts, round loaves of barley bread, piles of wheaten cakes, small sacks of corn, and platters of berries. There were jars of honey, as big as thimbles, and bottles of heather-ale, as big as acorns. Icicles and hailstones shone like diamonds among the branches, brightly coloured feathers and shells were fastened to the bark, and chains of frozen water-drops swung to and fro, reflecting the candle-light.

Through the tip-top of this wonderful tree gleamed the Christmas Star.

"What do you think of my tree?" asked Moldy Warp, stepping out of the shadows.

"Beau-u-u-tiful," they murmured.

"It's not a rose tree, nor a holly tree, nor an apple tree. Is it a Fairy Tree, Mole?" asked Grey Rabbit.

"It's a Christmas Tree," replied Mole in his soft mysterious voice. "It's for all the birds and beasts of the woods and fields. They will see it from afar and come here. Now sit quietly and watch."

Across the snowy fields padded little dark creatures, all filled with curiosity to see the glowing lights in the tree. Some were thin, and some were lame, and many were poor, for it had been a hard winter. With them romped the gay little rabbits, the squirrels and field mice. The family of Milkman Hedgehog trudged through the snowdrifts. The carollers and market people were there, and Water Rat in his brown velvet coat. Even Wise Owl flew down to see what was the matter, and Rat with his wife and baby stood on the edge of the crowd.

"Help yourselves," cried Mole, waving his short arms.

"It is Christmas. Eat and drink and warm yourselves.
Take away as much as you want for your store-rooms."

Then every little creature ate the good food, and
drank the sweet honeyed ale, and carried away little
bags and baskets of meal and cakes and corn. The birds
filled their knapsacks, the squirrels filled their pockets.
When they had finished there was nothing left except
the glowing candles which the wind could not extin-
guish. Mole had made them himself down underground,
where he kept his stores.

From behind a tree Rat sidled towards Grey Rabbit
and touched his hat.

"Miss Grey Rabbit," said he. "A word in your ear.
I found a scarlet sledge in the field last night, and my
Missis read your family name on it, so I took the liberty
of bringing it here for you."

"Oh, thank you, kind Rat!" cried Grey Rabbit,
clapping her paws with delight.

"My Missis helped me to drag it along," added Rat.
He took Grey Rabbit to the sledge and then without
waiting for more he hurried away to his family, who
peeped round the corner.

"The sledge is found! Come, Hare! Squirrel! Moldy
Warp! Wise Owl! Come and see our sledge," called
Grey Rabbit, and everyone crowded round to admire it.

The little scarlet sledge was clean and bright, for Rat
had rubbed the snow away. On the top was a fleecy
shawl covering something, and Grey Rabbit drew from

under it three objects, which she held up wonderingly.

The first was a walking-stick, made of peeled holly-wood, polished like ivory, and the handle was carved in the shape of Hare.

"That must be for me from good Santa Claus," said Hare, seizing it and swinging it about his head.

The second was a little wooden spoon with a hazel nut carved in the handle.

"That is certainly mine," said Squirrel and she put it in her pocket.

The third was a wee bone box, hanging on a string of berries, and when Grey Rabbit unfastened the lid there was a little white thimble inside which exactly fitted her.

"And I've never had a thimble since Wise Owl swallowed mine," said Grey Rabbit happily.

"Good Santa Claus," cried Hare. "He knew what we wanted. He has brought back our sledge filled with these things for us."

"Only one person could make such delicate carvings," said Grey Rabbit.

"And that is Rat," said Squirrel.

"They are peace offerings," suggested Mole.

"For Christmas-tide," added Old Hedgehog wisely.

"Three cheers for Rat!" cried Fuzzypeg, and they all cheered "Hip! Hip! Hurrah!"

Squirrel and Grey Rabbit climbed on the sledge, and Hare drew them over the snow.

"Good night. A happy Christmas!" they called, as

they left their friend behind.

"Too-whit, Too-whoo,

Merry Christmas to you," hooted Wise Owl as he sailed overhead, and flew across the wood to his own home in the beech tree. There could be no hunting for him on Christmas Day, but Mole's feast had helped him over the difficulty.

The sledge caught up with the little band of carollers, who sang as they marched along the lane. Their voices came clear and silvery through the air, and this is what Grey Rabbit heard:

"Holly red and mistletoe white,
    The stars are shining with golden light,
Burning like candles this Holy Night.
    Holly red and mistletoe white.

Mistletoe white and holly red,
    The doors are shut and the children a-bed.
Fairies at foot and angels at head.
    Mistletoe white and holly red."

"Heigh-o! I'm sleepy too," murmured Squirrel, "but it has been lovely! Thank you, Grey Rabbit, and Moldy Warp and Rat, and everyone for a happy day."

She curled down under the fleecy shawl by Grey Rabbit's side, and clutched her wooden spoon. Grey Rabbit sat wide awake on the swaying sledge, her thimble

was on her finger, her eyes shone with happiness.

"Peace on earth and mercy bright," her heart sang, and Hare ran swiftly over the frozen snow, drawing the scarlet-coloured sledge towards the little house at the end of the wood.

The End of the Story